The

Complete

Coby Collins

Marley Elementary Adventures

Volumes

1 – 5

Justin J

The Complete Coby Collins:

Marley Elementary Adventures

Volumes 1 – 5

Justin Johnson

I greatly appreciate you taking the time to read my work. Please consider leaving a review wherever you bought the book, or telling your friends or blog readers about this book, to help me spread the word.

Thank you for supporting my work.

This book is dedicated to the students of Fairgrieve Elementary, particularly those who took the trip through Jomoca Town!

and

To Duff, without whom there'd be no Coby.

CONTENTS

AUTHOR'S NOTE

What you are about to read can be found on my website. But, since a number of you may never make it to my website, I have chosen to include it in this book. It seems fitting, as this is the Complete story of Coby Collins, that I should include the mostly complete story of how Coby came about in the first place. I hope you enjoy it.

The Story

I'm a public school teacher. My career started with a group of 2nd graders in Fulton, NY.

As the year was drawing to a close, I thought, *Hey, I want to write a story for these guys!*

I went home and began working very hard on my first "book". It was called *Jomoca Island*, which was named after my classroom, *Jomoca Town.* The name Jomoca came from the three teachers who worked in the room. It was a very fun place to be!

Jomoca Island was a forty page masterpiece – at least for the kids in my class. It was about a kid going to a new school and how he was having difficulty adjusting to the idea. At the end of the book (***Spoiler Alert***), he ends up in our class, with all of the kids having a role in welcoming him.

The next year, I decided I wanted to write something a little different. I wanted to give my students a real story, but include a message. I wrote *Exception to the Rule*, which is – and will remain, unavailable to the public. My kids loved it, and some colleagues at work thought it was pretty cool – but it was too focused on driving the 'never give up' point home. Plus, it was wickedly derivative of Roald Dahl. I love Roald Dahl – but there's only one Roald Dahl, and that's the way it should be.

During the summer, just after the school year ended, I thought I would get a leg up on the next year's story. I bought a typewriter and set to work. I'd write ten pages here, five pages there. But all of my ideas felt flat and uninteresting.

Then my wife and I found out that a dear friend had passed away. We went to spend the days leading up to the funeral with his widow. We stayed in his house and spent the time reading his old books and rummaging through boxes, remembering fun and interesting things about him. His name was Dudley Leavitt. His friends called him "Duff".

As I was looking through some of Duff's things, I came across a story he'd written about a horse. It was clearly meant to be a picture book. But it was interesting. Along with the story, was a rejection letter from Simon & Schuster Publishers. I had no idea Duff had aspired to be a writer.

His story inspired me. I found a cozy corner of the house and started typing on my laptop. I didn't have much time, but with the time I did have, I wrote the Prologue to Coby Collins. My wife and I headed home after the funeral and I set up shop in the office – on my typewriter. For some reason I thought I was more creative if I used a typewriter. Weird, huh?

I wrote the first draft of Coby Collins. It was a stand-alone book at that time and it would be perfect for my next group of 2nd graders. Then I got the call...I would be teaching Kindergarten when I went back to school in the Fall.

I loved teaching Kindergarten – it was a lot of fun and very rewarding. But I couldn't give them my story...and I have no artistic talent, so I couldn't make them a picture book. So, Coby Collins sat in a pile on my desk, next to my typewriter. I thought that I had to do something with it, so I had it made into a book and gave it to friends and family.

I got the news last year (2014) that I would be teaching 2nd grade again, after three years of Kindergarten. I was very excited, but I'd almost forgotten about Coby Collins. And then a friend of mine, John Mercer, wrote and published a novel. It's called *They Call Me Zombie.* It's a very fun story and definitely worth checking out. I looked at his book and thought that it looked really professional. He self-published it, but his book didn't look like a *Self-*

Published book. It looked like a book you would find at the book store.

I thought, *I want to make one of those for my students.* And then I remembered Coby Collins. I spent most of the year trying to edit it and get it right...and since I used a typewriter, I had to copy it, word by word, into a computer document. It took forever! But, finally, after a few months it was done. I had the book made, but I didn't buy any copies. I wanted to make sure my students would like the story.

As April wound down and we headed into May, I read them the first book – from 8X11 sheets of paper that I'd printed from my home printer. They loved it! And they asked for more. So every night after work, I went home, made dinner, got the kids to bed...and wrote – for hours. It was like something out of *Shakespeare In Love.* I would bring a new chapter or two in and read it to my class and they would tell me to keep going and write more.

After two weeks I had another story. But something was different about this one. The ending. I hadn't planned on it, but it happened just the same. I had created a serialized fiction series. Each book leads into the next, like episodic television. The kids were thrilled with the story, but upset that I'd left them wanting, NO – needing to know what happens next.

So, I continued to write them. The fifth book is the final book in Coby's journey. That's not to say that there won't be any more Marley Elementary

Adventures, or a Fleshbot spin off...but Coby's story will be over.

It's been a long journey since that day, in the cozy little corner of our friend Duff's house. He would have liked Coby, I think. Give him a read. Maybe you'll like him too.

Justin Johnson

September 2014

COBY COLLINS

MARLEY ELEMENTARY
ADVENTURES
VOLUME ONE

JUSTIN JOHNSON

Contents

PROLOGUE

We were running as fast as we could, but nothing seemed fast enough to get away from these things. I was running out of breath.

The end of the tunnel was getting closer. It was dark but I could see a light up ahead.

"Come on Coby!"

Antoine was way ahead of me. I knew he was going to make it, but if I wasn't able to catch my breath they were going to catch me.

As we got closer to the end of the tunnel I saw something come into focus. From that far away it was difficult to see what it was. Within seconds Antoine had reached it. I had to wipe the sweat from my eyes and squint to tell that he was beginning to climb a ladder made of rope.

"Antoine, where do you think that ladder leads?" I hollered, severely out of breath.

"You mean you don't know?" Antoine yelled back.

"What?"

I kept running and was stunned at what I saw when I got there. Antoine was already up the ladder and safe...well, safer than I was.

I looked up and then I took one last glance back to see where they were.

That was a mistake.

GREEN ONION

CREAM CHEESE BREATH

I could hear them yelling at me. I could smell their breath and it wasn't pleasant. One of them said, "Get up!" I thought that was kind of weird, but that's what she said: "Get up!"

And the breath! Did I mention the breath these things had? It smelled like green onion cream cheese. Now, I happen to like green onion cream cheese. But I do not want it breathed in my face, under any circumstance.

I looked up the ladder for a sign of Antoine, but he wasn't there anymore. He must've gone to look for help. I'd like to think that if I was ever in the position to save my friend or go and save myself, I would choose to stay and get my friend out of trouble. But being the slow, fat kid, I will never be in that position.

They were upon me now and I could smell them stronger than ever. It was that same cream cheese breath, but now it was mixed with my sister's hairspray. Something didn't feel right.

"Get up! Come on Coby! Honestly, you're going to make us late for school – again! I almost have perfect attendance in the bag and you're not going to ruin it for me."

My sister stormed out of my bedroom, ripping the covers from my bed and throwing them onto the floor as she left.

I found myself wanting to go back to sleep to face the beast. Anything was better than my sister Jill. She was the pits. She's an absolutely wonderful person...as long as you're above the age of ten, which, sadly enough, I am not. She is also probably the smartest girl in the whole entire school.

I managed to rush and get ready before Jill got too mad. I got on the bus just in time to hear her tell the bus driver, and all of her friends, that we'd have been on the bus a lot earlier if I hadn't taken my 'sweet little time' getting ready.

I made my way to the back of the bus and the gang was all in their usual spots. There was me, Antoine, Davey, Tommy, Messins (he's a slob), and Fat Boy (I'd be Fat Boy if it wasn't for him).

On this particular day, Antoine brought in this toy that his parents had bought for him the night before. His parents were always buying him something so he'd shut his yap.

Antoine's my best friend. I mean, the gangs the gang, but me and Antoine go together like toads and warts.

He started telling us about his new toy.

"Guys, check this out!" he said. "It's the new Fleshbot. My parents got it for me last night if I promised to shut up. Which I did. No easy feat, I might add."

The gang oogled...every last one of 'em. "Wow, that's cool man," said Davey. "Yeah, dude," echoed Tommy. Messins was too busy wiping the jelly from a donut off of his shirt to comment, but he grunted his approval. Fat Boy was eating the rest of the donut Messins had started and with a full mouth said, "Wow, cool dude."

"That's right boys," Antoine started up again, "check out the way his head spins into his back to reveal a second, robotic head."

I've never been a huge fan of the Fleshbots, but the guys love them.

We heard the hissing sound the bus brakes make each morning when we get to school and we knew our chat was over for the time being.

A LITTLE TINGLE,
A BIG DOWNER

The morning seemed to drag more than normal. I didn't know if it was the fact that I was dreading the lunchtime conversation about Fleshbots, or that Mrs. Tingledowner seemed more boring than usual. Whatever it was, I found myself staring out the window and daydreaming. This wouldn't have been a problem but Mrs. Tingledowner seemed to be calling on me - alot.

"Coby, what's the product of three times three?" she asked.

Now, I'm not very good at math. I barely learned my addition and subtraction facts, let alone my multiplication and division. And this math at 9:15 in the morning didn't make things any easier.

"Um," I said. I just needed a minute to think.

"Oh, for heaven's sake, will somebody please help Coby out?" She paused for a minute to give everyone the chance to look in my direction.

"Antoine," she continued, "could you by any chance help your friend solve this pathetically easy math fact?"

Of course, he was able to tell her the answer was nine. Why couldn't I have done that? I mean really, it wasn't rocket science was it?

Thank goodness we had a small break after math. I needed some time to catch my breath and clear my mind. I went to my bag to get my snack only to discover that my parents had forgotten to pack it. I went to Mrs. Tingledowner to see if she had any food she could spare. She immediately asked me what ten times seven was. I didn't know the answer.

"Well, Mr. Collins, I really don't feel as though you deserve a snack. Do you?"

"My parents forgot-"

"Too bad, Mr. Collins," she said. Antoine came over to see if I was okay.

"Hey man," he said. "Do you want some of mine?"

"Yeah," I said. "Thanks."

"How could you not know the answer to three times three?" He looked at me with a little smirk, which quickly went away when he saw how upset I was. "I'm really sorry about that," he said. "Don't worry about her. She's got it out for everybody."

"She wasn't too mean to you was she?" I said.

"I got lucky today. Tomorrow might be different."

"Somehow I don't think it will be."

"Hey, listen," he said, "just hang in there. And whatever you do, don't do anything stupid."

*****

Reading came just after snack.

"Coby," Mrs. Tingledowner asked, "who is the main character in this story?"

I looked down at my book, suddenly aware that I was three pages behind the rest of the class. I hadn't turned past the title page. I was done now. I didn't know who the main character in the story was. I didn't know who any of the characters in the story were.

"I don't know who the main character is," I said.

"Well," she said, "that's because you haven't so much as bothered to even look at your book! Have you? Can you answer that question, Coby? Have you even looked at your book?"

"No, Mrs. Tingledowner, I haven't."

I might have been fine with this, normally. But the way today had gone, I felt myself start to snap.

"It's about time - " she started before I interrupted her.

"About time what?" I asked without giving her time to respond. "About time I got an answer correct? About time I answered without making a complete fool out of myself?"

"Mr. Collins, you'd better control yourself or you'll be headed to the principal's office. And when he's done with you, I'll have you for a nice long detention."

"I really don't mind going to see Mr. Flannery. He's actually kind of nice to the kids, even if they are in trouble. You could learn something from him!"

It became very apparent to me that the other kids were watching us. There was no backing down now.

"Get out, Mr. Collins! Get out!"

"If that's what you really want," I said, not knowing when to give up. "If you really want me to go to the office so Mr. Flannery can show me how a grown up is supposed to act, I will."

With that I left the room. Somehow, I thought going to the office would be better than the remaining time left in the morning with Mrs. Tingledowner.

I was wrong.

THE OFFICE

It was a long walk to the office. I had time to think about what I'd just done. I began to sweat. I was in big trouble. I had never actually been to the principal's office before but I didn't think it could be that bad.

I was nervous. I decided to go to the bathroom before heading down to the office. I find that this is always best when you're nervous – not just about going to the office, but about anything really. I find that I usually have to pee very badly and, well, the bathroom is certainly the place to do that.

When I arrived at the office there was a tall lady with gray hair and glasses hanging on the tip of her nose. She was looking through her glasses at me in a way that made me feel like I'd done something wrong – besides the obvious.

"Are you Coby Collins?" she asked.

I noticed just how many people there were in there. I took a quick look around to see if I would at least have a chair to sit in when she was done with her questioning. I didn't see one.

"Yes, I am," I finally said.

"Well," she said looking around at all the other students who had found their way to the office this morning "you will be heading directly in to see

Principal Flannery because of the severity of what you've done."

I followed Mrs. 'Hanging Glasses' toward the door that attached Mr. Flannery's office to the main office.

The first thing I noticed when I entered Mr. Flannery's office was how bad it smelled. It was the perfect mixture of sweat and fear.

"Smell that my boy?" Mr. Flannery said, not bothering to look away from the book he was reading.

"Smell what?" I asked. I didn't want to seem rude about the terrible smell in his office. I wasn't even sure if he smelled it himself.

"Smell what?" he parroted back in a mocking tone. "The smell of those who've come before you, of course."

He stood up now and slammed the book on the desk and I noticed that Mr. Flannery was a very large man. He towered over me and looked straight down.

He was bald and wore glasses. He had a very full and bushy beard that looked a little strange on his round face.

"That's right Coby, those who've come before you." He looked down at me smiling. "I see that you're already sweating, so the person who comes in next will smell a little bit of you too."

I wiped my forehead with my sleeve. This guy was creeping me out. I was hoping that this would be over soon so I could go back to Mrs. Tingledowner's class.

"Coby," Mr. Flannery said, "do you want to tell me about what happened in class this morning?"

I looked down at my shoes. I didn't want to tell him. I had just met him and it didn't seem like telling him about this morning would make a very good first impression.

"I already know what happened," he said. "I know what you did." The look of surprise on my face must have amused him. He continued, "Every teacher in this school has a little phone in their classroom. All the teacher has to do is pick up this phone and dial 'o.' Then they get to talk to me."

"If you already know what I did, why do you need me to tell you about it?" I asked.

"It's important that you tell me, so that you take responsibility for your actions?"

I told him everything. It was my only way out of there. I felt humiliated. I was embarrassed by what I'd done.

"Was that so difficult?" he asked.

I wanted to tell him that it was, but all I said was, "No, that wasn't so difficult."

SUZY TRUDELL

I got to go back to class just in time to go to lunch. Antoine asked what happened in Mr. Flannery's office. I told him that nothing happened and that Flannery was okay.

"Really?" he asked. "I hadn't heard that about him at all.   You know Suzy?"

"Suzy Singer?"

"No," he said, "Suzy Trudell."

"Yeah," I said, "I know her. Fifth grade right? My sister can't stand her 'cause she's always in trouble."

"That's true. I heard that she was down in Flannery's office just last week because she plugged the toilet in the girls' bathroom."

"What's the big deal about that?" I asked. "If I got in trouble every time I plugged a toilet I'd never see the light of day."

"Yeah, but she didn't plug it naturally," Antoine said. "She balled up a big wad of paper towels and put them in there just to see if the water would overflow."

"Did it?" I asked.

"How do you think she got caught?"

"Where are you going with this?" I said. "It doesn't mean that Flannery's a bad guy."

"Your're right," he said looking around, "but what he did to her does."

"What are you talking about?"

"I'll have to tell you later." We were at the cafeteria already. There was to be no talking of such things in the cafeteria – ever!

Our lunch monitor, Mrs. Poley, was a tough nut to crack. She never smiled and it seemed to most of us that if she were to ever crack a smile that her whole face might crack as well. "GET YOUR LUNCH! SIT DOWN! SHUT UP!" bellowed Mrs. Poley.

"Well a good afternoon to you too," said Antoine, under his breath.

*****

The 'catch of the day' was tuna surprise and the old standby, a peanut butter and jelly sandwich made on old crusty bread, packed in a tight plastic wrapper. Normally, I liked peanut butter and jelly, but when it sits in that stinky old plastic all morning it starts to taste like the plastic. It's pretty disgusting.

I remembered that my parents didn't pack me anything to eat today. Crusty, plastic tasting peanut butter and jelly it was.

When I sat down at the table I noticed that Tommy and Davey were eating ham and swiss sandwiches that their moms had made them. I saw Messins trying frantically to wipe the mustard from his bologna sandwich off of his pants. The whole time he's yelling, "My mom's gonna kill me! My mom's gonna kill me!" Fat Boy looked like he had an eight course meal in front of him; sandwiches and cookies and pies and chips and pudding. Surprisingly enough, there were no fruits or vegetables.

Antoine and I had a seat at the end of the table and began to eat our lunch in silence, as was the rule.

The peanut butter was a new low as far as I was concerned. It tasted like sticky cardboard. Antoine had chosen the tuna surprise, and surprise...it was lousy. He took two bites and pushed it aside.

I was hoping that Antoine would get back to the Suzy Trudell story, but he decided to talk about the Fleshbots with Tommy and Davey instead. I wasn't really interested, so I only half listened to what they were saying.

"Oh man, Antoine that's so cool. You're parents are awesome! My parents were going to get me one, but then they said that I shouldn't be playing with anything that can change into a robot and destroy the world." Tommy was drooling over his sandwich.

"Well," said Davey, "my parents bought me all the Fleshbot toys last night. I mean everything. Pandora and Lenny and Zenu and Globar and all of them! They even got me their secret lair."

"You're such a liar!" said Tommy.

"No, I'm not," Davey defended himself. "I'm telling the truth, I swear."

"Yeah?" said Antoine. "Did you even know that they haven't made the lair yet?

Davey looked dumbstruck.

Antoine didn't even give him a chance to answer. "No, you didn't know that, because if you had, then you would never have opened your big fat mouth in the first place."

Most of the conversation was like this. The only thing I heard that was of any interest to me at all was that when the Fleshbots are angry and don't want to fully change into robots, they will turn their eyes red while they are still in human form. They only do it for a second - just long enough to get out their anger without letting the regular humans see them. I thought this seemed cool.

When lunch was finally over we made our way back up to the classroom for our social studies lesson.

Mrs. Tingledowner gave me a fake little smile when I entered the room. I took my seat and told myself that I didn't want to end up back in Flannery's office if I could help it. I would do whatever she said and take everything with a smile on my face, no matter what.

"Now," she started our lesson, "can anyone tell me something that Squanto showed the Pilgrims how to do? Something he taught them to do so they could survive the winters in the New World?"

She waited for a second and I was relieved when she picked Derek Snider instead of me. He answered.

"Well done Derrick, that's correct." She gave him a little wink that just about made me puke on my desk.

"Now, can anyone tell me what kinds of houses they lived in? And how were they able to keep them warm all through the winter?"

This was the one. I could feel it. I didn't know the correct answer and so, of course, she would call on me.

"Joanna, could you help us with this one?"

I was shocked. The rest of the lesson went by and Mrs. Tingledowner didn't call on me once. That's not to say she didn't give me dirty looks from time to time. But, when it was all said and done, I felt pretty good about the situation and what the rest of the day had in store for me –until it was time to go to gym.

UN-SPECIAL SPECIAL

"Class," Mrs. Tingledowner said, "it's time to go to gym. Please line up."

As we lined up her eyes caught mine. "Not you Coby. I have other plans for you." I looked at Antoine, unsure what to do.

"Do what she says," he said.

"Coby," Mrs. Tingledowner said, "you will take this spot, right here, in the front of the line."

It was pretty embarrassing to be in the front of the line when everyone knew I was in a heap of trouble. Normally, the front of the line is the spot everyone wants. I'd have been perfectly happy with the end of the line today.

She dropped everyone off at the gym. I got to stand there outside the door and watch all of my friends go in without me.

When the last student had gone in, Mrs. Tingledowner grabbed me by the wrist and led me to the office. You don't realize how fast your teachers can walk until they're angry with you.

The lady with the funny looking glasses was still behind the counter when we got there.

"I need to use the phone Doris, if you would?" Mrs. Tingledowner said. Doris, I thought to myself, she looked like a Doris.

Mrs. Tingledowner picked up the phone and started dialing my number.

"Hello, Mr. Collins?" she said speaking into the phone, the whole time glaring down at me. "This is Mrs. Tingledowner from Marley Elementary School. I have your son, Coby, with me in the office."

She was silent for a moment. I could tell my father was talking.

"Oh, no, he's okay." I'm not sure if that was entirely true. "He just had a little incident with me today in the classroom and I was wondering if it would be okay with you if I kept him tonight after school for some extra work on his math facts?

"Yes...mhmm...yes. I see. Tomorrow will be fine then. Thank you for your time Mr. Collins. Okay...you too...bye."

She hung up the phone and wheeled around on me. Her eyes seemed to be staring right through me. This was not the same woman who just got off the phone with my father, was it?

"Well Coby, it turns out your sister's birthday is today. Therefore, you are going out to celebrate with your family tonight. Tomorrow night, however, you and I will be working extra hard. For now you are free to go to Gym and I will pencil you in for our little appointment tomorrow."

I just stared at her. I didn't know what it meant to be 'penciled in,' but it sounded important.

Before I turned to leave I saw the strangest thing. I didn't believe it at first, but it seemed too real not to be true. Maybe I'd been spending too much time with Antoine, but I could've sworn that I saw her eyes glow red. It was only for a second, and it wasn't very bright. But they were red. I was sure they were.

THE TACO JOINT

Getting home that night was like a blur to me. It was a rush to get my coat off, drop my bag, go to the bathroom, wash my hands, get my coat back on, and head for the car to go to the restaurant.

We were going to The Taco Joint, which was my sister's favorite restaurant of all time. I hated the place, and not just because she liked it. I hated it because Mexican food always seemed to give me a stomach ache that doesn't go away until the next day. I just hate tacos and fajitas and burritos and beans and rice and guacamole and salsa. I hate it all.

As I expected it was awful. The food was too spicy and my parents were so nice to my sister. I know it was her birthday, but come on already. Enough was enough.

All of these things were bothering me, but what really had its grip on my mind were those glowing eyes of Mrs. Tingledowner. I couldn't seem to get that look of hers out of my head. It was like lasers burning into my brain.

"Hey spaz! What are you doing?" Jill caught me daydreaming.

"I'm thinking," I said.

"Oh, wow, I didn't think you were capable of that Mr. What's three-times-three?" She said with a giant smirk in my direction.

"How'd you hear about that?" I asked.

"I have my sources," she said.

"Come on, Jill." my mother said. "Leave Coby alone please."

"But mom, this is so much fun...and it is my birthday."

She saw that my mother was serious. "Oh, alright," she finally agreed.

After dinner it was time for dessert. Jill loved fried ice cream, so instead of a birthday cake, she had fried ice cream with a candle in it. I hate fried ice cream, and I just wanted dinner to be over as soon as possible, so I didn't eat anything.

When we got home I went to bed. I couldn't stop seeing Tingledowner's red eyes staring at me. I couldn't stop seeing her smiling just before her head swung back and revealed a robot's head. I woke up and looked at my alarm clock: 3 AM. I still had the next four hours to try to sleep and I was covered in sweat from having nightmares about my teacher turning into a Fleshbot.

One thing was clear to me. I had to tell Antoine as early as possible tomorrow. I also had to find out what happened to Suzy Trudell.

CONFIDING IN A FRIEND

The bus couldn't come fast enough for me the next day. When I got on, I noticed that Antoine was sitting in his usual seat. He was playing with his latest Fleshbot toy. Seeing it in his hands sent a shiver through my body.

"Hey," Antoine said.

"We've gotta talk," I said. Antoine looked at me like I was acting a little crazy. "And you've gotta put that toy away, where I can't see it, okay?"

"Why?"

"Because when I talk to you I don't want to look at it!"

"Jeez," he said, "alright."

He put the toy in his backpack and gave me a puzzled look.

"What do you need to talk about?" he asked.

"I want to talk to you about something that happened to me yesterday with Mrs. Tingledowner."

"That again," he said. "Forget about it, Coby."

"Come on," I begged. "Hear me out, would ya?"

"Okay," he said.

I did a quick check over the seat and into the aisle to make sure that nobody else was listening.

"I think Mrs. Tingledowner is one of those things," I whispered.

The look on his face told me he didn't understand.

"You know," I said, "a Fleshbot."

"What?" he said. His eyes got huge. "Are you out of your mind?"

"No Antoine, I mean it. I don't even like those things," I said. "But I do know that they have red eyes, right?"

"Yeah. So what's that have to do with Mrs. Tingledowner?"

I looked over the seat and into the aisle again. This was stuff I didn't want anyone but Antoine to hear. He was already thinking that I was nuts, what would the other kids say?

"Yesterday in the office," I said, "while you guys were at Gym, she called my father. When she got off the phone she looked right at me like she was really mad and wanted to rip my head off or something."

"You helped with that," he said.

"I understand that," I said, "but when she looked at me her eyes turned red just like one of the Fleshbots."

"Coby," Antoine was yelling now, "they're not real. They are one hundred percent made up!"

"If you don't believe me that's fine," I said. "Just let me ask you one more question. What do they do when they're really mad at someone and they want to hurt them, or whatever it is they do?"

"They take them to their secret lair and hold them captive while they decide if the person is worthy of becoming one of them," he told me. "They put them through a series of tests. If they can handle it, they convert them to a Fleshbot and send them out into their community to recruit more humans for the Fleshbot Legion."

"What kinds of tests?" I asked.

"They try to find out how tough a person is," Antoine said. "Sometimes they pull their hair, other times they laser beam their legs; sometimes they grab their arms really hard and lead them around by the wrist. It's really painful and leaves quite a bruise."

The bus came to a lurching stop. I was just getting ready to ask Antoine to tell me what happened to Suzy Trudell in Mr. Flannery's office. Suzy was waiting at the bus stop though, and I could already see it. I didn't have to ask.

SUZY REVISITED

Suzy Trudell was sent home a week earlier. Everyone knew that. What they didn't know was why, exactly. I'd heard rumors about her getting lippy with her teacher, or not getting her homework done on time, or plugging the toilets with paper towels. She was a bad girl and everyone knew it.

"Do you see that?" I asked Antoine. It was clear by the look on his face that he had. He looked as stunned as everyone else.

As Suzy stepped onto the bus we could hear gasps coming from every direction. Her hair had been chopped off. Not completely, but definitely enough to be noticeable. It was cut jaggedly, like the person who'd cut it hadn't cared what it looked like when they'd finished.

I could tell by the way Suzy was covering her face with her books that she cared. It was also clear by the way her parents were standing in the doorway that there had been an argument about whether she would go to school.

"Antoine," I said, "tell me what you heard yesterday."

He looked at me and said, "I didn't hear much. I heard that he screamed at her..."

"What else did you hear?" I followed up.

"Just that he made her sit in the corner of his office while he yelled at the other kids. He made her just sit there staring at the wall. And when she asked if she could get up and go, he took the chair away from her and he made her stand there all afternoon before she got sent home on a private bus."

"That may have happened," I said, "but there was a lot more that happened in that office yesterday, that's for sure."

Suzy was walking by us now, going to take her usual seat in the back of the bus. As she walked by me she moved her left hand through her chopped off hair and her sleeve dropped away to reveal a hand shaped bruise on her wrist.

"I've gotta find out what happened to her," I said looking back to Antoine.

"Don't do it," he said. "This is none of your business."

He may have been right, but something was going on here.

And I, Coby Collins, was going to find out what it was.

THE PLAN

My game plan for the day was pretty simple. I was going to lay low and try not to get into trouble. Well, more trouble than I was already in. I was also going to try to follow Mrs. Tingledowner around the building during lunch and art class. I remembered that Antione had mentioned something about a secret lair that the Fleshbots had. I knew it was a stretch, but maybe they had a secret lair in our school. I had to follow her to try to find out where this lair might be.

I would have to be very careful if I didn't want to end up like poor Suzy Trudell. I also had to find out what really happened to her.

The first part of the plan went by without a hitch. I sat through class and paid attention and answered Mrs. Tingledowner as politely as I could. It was on the way to lunch that the real challenges would start.

"Listen Antoine," I said, "I'm going to sneak out of the line before we go downstairs. If anyone asks, you don't know where I am, okay?"

"No Coby. Don't do this!" He was begging. It was nice to know that he wanted me to do the right thing and keep myself out of trouble. But I have to be honest, all his 'goody-two-shoes' stuff and his doubting me was really getting old.

"Quit being a baby about everything," I said, "and just do this for me, would ya?"

"No."

I was getting upset. I'm the one that helped him last year when he got into that fight with Glen Davis. Do you think he could return the favor?

"Come on-" I said.

"What do we have here?"

Busted.

I had managed to make it all morning without getting into a lick of trouble and now that I was trying to do something really sneaky, Mrs. Tingledowner was all over me. We weren't even out of the room yet.

"Mr. Collins," she said, "and his best friend Antoine." She turned to the other students to make sure they were all paying attention. She waited for just a beat before beginning again. "Talking at the end of our line? Holding us up from getting our lunch and keeping us from a well-deserved break? What do you think about that, children?"

The other kids in the class took turns giving us dirty looks. I looked at Antoine and noticed that he was staring at me along with the other kids. Mrs. Tingledowner wasn't finished either. "Do us all a favor, would you...shut up!"

We were walking down the hall and I had no idea what Antoine was going to do. I couldn't count on him. I had to do this myself.

As the class headed down the stairs I ducked into a doorway to an unused broom closet. The door was closed and locked, but the doorway was deep enough that nobody could see me. I saw Antoine take one final look back with a very sour look on his face, like he was angry that I went through with it and that he had no idea where I was going.

Once the class was out of sight I ran to the other end of the building as fast as I could, trying desperately not to be seen by anybody. When I got to the stairway on that side of the building I went down very carefully, hoping Mrs. Tingledowner was still over by the cafeteria. If she was, then I could hide underneath the stairwell until she came down.

I was trying not to look like I was sneaking down the stairs because there were a lot of other teachers around. I had to be careful not to be seen by any of them.

"Hello Coby," a familiar voice said from behind me.

It was Mrs. Donnely, my teacher from last year. She was just finishing up her lunch and heading back to her room.

"Hi," I said.

"How's third grade going?" she asked.

Why is it that whenever you talk to an adult they always want to know how your current grade is going? I know they're just trying to be nice, but do you think they could ever just say 'hello' and be on their way?

"It's going fine," I lied.

I've found that if you don't want to spend a lot of time talking to somebody all you need to do is keep your answers short and positive. They almost always say 'that's great' and then continue on their way.

"That's great," she said, "what's your favorite thing about this year?"

It almost always works, unless you're trying to sneak off during lunch to catch your teacher doing something evil!

For these cases you have to think quickly.

"Listen," I said, "Mrs. Donnely, I'd love to talk to you all day, but if I don't get to the bathroom, I'm going to poop my pants right here in the hallway."

"Well you'd better go then," she said. She ran upstairs very quickly.

That's another thing I've found out. If you tell someone that you have to go to the bathroom, especially poop, they don't want anything to do with you. These are very handy pieces of information to have in the back of your mind.

It was nice that I said 'poop' because now I didn't even have to pretend to go to the bathroom. Mrs. Donnely was gone so fast that I was able to sneak behind the stairwell before Mrs. Tingledowner could to get to this side of the building.

It was disgusting underneath the stairs. Cobwebs and dead bugs littered the floor, and at my eye level I could see wads of chewing gum that some of the older students had probably placed there after it'd lost its flavor.

I knew I had to stay under here though. If I didn't, then I risked getting caught. I was already in enough trouble.

I started to notice the smell. It was kind of a nasty smell that made me wish that Mrs. Tingledowner would hurry up already. It smelled like vomit mixed with dead, decaying worms. The smell that happens after it rains and all the worms come to the surface and settle on top of the ground. Some of them make it and some of them don't, and the ones that don't really seem to leave an utterly disgusting smell.

I was pretty relieved when I saw Mrs. Tingledowner step into the office. I still couldn't move, but at least she was down in this end of the building. I saw her getting her mail and talking with some of the other teachers. Mr. Flannery came out of his office to talk to her and I was able to hear what they were saying.

"Are you going down today?" he asked her.

"Yes, I'll be down in about a minute," she said.

"I can't right now," he said, "I have this pesky little nuisance to take care of at the moment." He looked in the direction of a first grader named Gerry Dunham, who had a large amount of what looked like green paint on his shirt.

"I see," said Mrs. Tingledowner, "maybe we can meet later." With that she gave him a wink and he gave her a wink and then she left the office.

Creeping very slowly I was able to get my head to the point that I could see around the stairs. I noticed that Mrs. Tingledowner did not go into the 'Staff Lounge' like the other teachers.

She just walked by. When a few other teachers asked, "Aren't you eating with us today, Devindra?" she just looked past them and kept walking. I thought she was just going to head back upstairs to the classroom, but she didn't do that at all. Looking back on it now, I wish she had. Instead, she went through a door I'd never noticed before.

*****

It was a plain door, painted light brown to match all of the other doors in the school. It looked to be made of metal and had no window whatsoever. It had a very small sign toward the top, perfectly centered, which read:

Teachers Only
No Students Past This Point

I had to think of a reason to get into that room. I couldn't just walk in and act like I belonged there. If Mrs. Tingledowner caught me down at this end of the school without my lunch or a nurse's pass then I'd be done. And then it came to me: My reason for being down at this end of the school during lunch hour without a pass would be...I forgot my lunch money.

I had to face it – I was a goner. But I just had to find out what was behind that door. How would I be able to live with myself if I went home without looking. Or worse; if I went to detention and had no idea what this secret place was that Mrs. Tingledowner was going to on her lunch break.

I just did it. I was more scared than I'd ever been. The lump in my throat was huge, the sweat beaded on my forehead, and I'm pretty sure my knees were shaking. But I did it anyway. I reached out my hand and opened the door.

And when I had mustered up enough courage to open my eyes and look at what was inside this magical room, what did I see?

It was just a square room a few feet wide and a few feet long. Mrs. Tingledowner was gone.

I noticed two things. There was a trap door in the floor and a large hook that hung on the wall. I had a feeling I knew where Mrs. Tingledowner was, but I would have to wait until later to find out. It was just too dangerous to try to find out now. She could quite possibly be down there waiting for me to make a mistake.

Instead, I went back to lunch. Mrs. Poley was not very pleased with me.

I sat down next to Antoine and told him what I'd seen. He didn't believe me and thought I should just try to keep myself out of trouble.

I would just have to find a way to show Antoine that I was serious, that the room I saw existed and there was something hidden underneath that door in the floor. And that Mrs. Tingledowner was down there doing something and it was probably something evil. And that Mr. Flannery knew about this place too. They had spoken about it. I'd have to prove it to him.

But how?

BETWEEN LUNCH AND PART THREE

It was ten minutes after lunch and we were still waiting for Mrs. Tingledowner. It wasn't like her to be this late and we could tell that Mrs. Poley was getting mad.

We'd never seen her face so red. She was so mad at Mrs. Tingledowner that she'd completely forgotten about us. She just stared at the clock, letting us talk and walk around the room and do whatever we wanted. It was like she'd just given up.

"Seriously, Coby," Antoine said looking around so no one would hear. "You tell me that you think our teacher is evil – not just evil, a Fleshbot. And then you tell me that our principal, good old Mr. Flannery, might be one too."

He was right.

"And then on top of this," he said, "you tell me there's a secret room inside the school, or perhaps underneath the school. You sound nuts! Do you expect me to believe this?"

I gave it a second to sink in and really give it some thought. "Yeah," I said.

Antoine rolled his eyes and started to walk away from me. I followed him. "Tell me everything you know about the Fleshbots." I said. A few of the boys had overheard this and started to laugh.

"What do you want to know?" Antoine said, looking very annoyed.

"I don't know. Anything really," I said.

He gave me a quick look and then looked up at the clock. "Okay," he said, "talk to me during our break before art today. I'll tell you as much as I know."

"Great. Thanks," I said.

As I turned to walk away he grabbed me by the arm.

"Don't think this means I'm helping you with Tingledowner and Flannery," he said.

"I know," I said. But I didn't really care. I was going to get all of the information I needed in about a half an hour. Antoine didn't need to know what I was going to do with it.

*****

At break time I walked over to Antoine and asked him again to tell me everything he knew about the Fleshbots.

"Okay, first thing you gotta know," he said, "is their eyes go red when they're really mad, but not mad enough to turn into a robot. Got it?"

I nodded that I understood so we could move on.

"Second," he continued, "when they do turn into a robot, their head and part of their back are the only things that change." I gave him a puzzled look, so he elaborated. "You know that on the toys the heads flip back into the body and out comes the robot, right?"

"Yes."

"When the robot head comes out of the back it also brings out a metal strip that replaces the part of their back that went inside."

"Alright," I said, "so when does the rest of it change?"

"It doesn't," he said, "How many times have you been over to my house to watch the show or play with my toys?"

"A lot," I said, "but I never really paid that much attention before."

He had a look of disappointment after I said this. He'd been trying to get me into the Fleshbots for a whole year. I guess the fact that I hadn't been paying attention hurt his feelings.

"Well then," he said after a few long seconds, " I think you know all of the basics. That should be enough for today. Not that you've been paying attention anyway." He turned around and walked back to his desk and took out a book.

Great, I thought, now I have two major problems: A teacher who's a Fleshbot and a best friend who won't talk to me.

The worst thing of all was that I didn't get all of the information I thought I was going to need.

One thing was for certain – I would have to see what that underground room looked like before the day was over. And, if I could, show Antoine that I was telling the truth.

It took me the entire Social Studies lesson to figure it out. I knew how I would show Antoine the lair.

I would skip Art, just as I had done with lunch.

The next part of the plan called for me to go to the Computer Lab and talk to Mrs. Giga about the school's digital camera. It wasn't uncommon for Mrs. Tingledowner to send a student down to borrow it.

I had never been asked, but as far as I could tell Mrs. Giga wasn't too strict about who she gave the camera to. I would just tell her that Mrs. Tingledowner needed to take pictures of a lesson we were doing, and that she needed the camera as soon as she could get it, and that she was sorry she didn't give Mrs. Giga more notice. It would be a piece of cake.

The last part of my plan was the most daring. It involved me taking the camera and going down to the secret room all by myself. At least, I hoped I would be by myself.

Once I got down there I would take as many pictures as I could. It was at this point of the plan that I realized I was not going to be able to show Antoine the pictures until he got home. I was pretty sure he was my only hope for surviving detention.

MRS. GIGA

When it came time to line up it was very easy to avoid Antoine. I went to the back of the line and, since he still wasn't talking to me, he asked one of his other friends at the front of the line to let him cut.

It was also easy to get away from the class since Mrs. Tingledowner always walked in the front of the line facing the direction we were going. She simply trusted that her wretchedness would be enough to make us behave. Most of the time it worked – but not today.

As they turned right I went left down the forbidden sixth grade hallway. I had never been down here before. It wasn't as scary as I thought it would be. The kids were all in their classrooms paying attention.

I kind of liked how quiet it was. I actually thought about staying there for a while, but I had to get to Mrs. Giga's room and get that camera. I didn't think it would be too difficult.

I was hoping that Mrs. Giga was as big a push over as everyone had told me.

*****

She wasn't.

"Coby," she said, "what are you doing down here? Aren't you supposed to be in Art class?"

This was not happening. How in the world did she know my schedule?

"Yes, I am," I said.

"Well then," she said, "shouldn't you be on your way there now?"

"Actually, Mrs. Giga," I said, "Ms. Flo sent me down to borrow the camera."

She looked at me suspiciously, "I think I'm going to have to call her and make sure."

I was done now.

She picked up the phone and dialed Ms. Flo's number.

She waited and then looked at me. I was trying to look like this was what I'd expected all along.

"It's ringing," she said.

One ring...I could hear...two rings...three rings...and then, "Hello, Ms. Flo? Sorry to disturb your class. I have Coby Collins here. Yes, I know he should be in your room. He said that you needed the camera today, is that correct?"

She gave me a rather harsh look and then continued, "I see, okay. Well thank you for clearing things up. I'll send him right down." Mrs. Giga hung up the phone and then glared at me. "It seems, Mr. Collins, that Ms. Flo did not need the camera. In fact, she didn't even send you. What do you have to say about that?"

I didn't have anything to say.

"Nothing?" she said, "Well in that case," she turned around and started walking to the other side of the room, "I have no choice but to send you back to Ms. Flo with the camera in hand."

Opening her desk drawer, she pulled out the camera, checked to make sure it had memory card, and handed it to me. I stared at her for a moment. She gave me a wink and then went over to shut the door to the computer lab.

"I can imagine you're quite confused," she said.

"Yes. I mean, I thought..."

"I know what you thought," she said, "I just had to make sure that you were doing this on your own."

"Doing what on my own?" I asked.

She walked to the back of the lab and waved her hand for me to follow. We crouched in the back row below the windows and behind a group of computers.

"Your assumptions, young man, are the same as mine," she said, "although, I could never attempt to prove them correct."

"Excuse me," I said, "but what are you talking about?"

"You know as well as I do that you were not getting that camera for art class. Now, I didn't actually talk to Ms. Flo," she said, "I avoid that at all costs. I find her to be rather annoying. I merely pretended to call her to see how you would react. You see, if you would have been here to get the camera, as you said, from her room with her permission, then when I made the phone call you would have been perfectly fine with it and you wouldn't have squirmed as much as you did. However, you were not sent by her, so even though I was pretending to be on the phone with her, you looked a bit anxious...and I'm being nice when I say 'a bit.'"

So she hadn't called Ms.Flo. I was relieved about that, but I still had no idea what on earth she was talking about.

"I can see you're still confused," she continued, "Let me ask you this: Do you think there's something strange about your teacher?"

"Mrs. Tingledowner?" I asked.

"Who else would I be talking about?" She was starting to lose her patience with me. "Haven't you noticed," she said, "that when she gets angry her eyes turn a bright shade of red?"

"Yeah. Why? Have you?"

"I wouldn't have asked you if I hadn't," she said. "I've been after Tingledowner for years."

"Why are you telling me all of this?" I asked.

"Because I need your help and you need mine," she said. "I'm going to give you the camera and you are going to get to that place under the school that you saw this morning."

I looked at her, stunned. I couldn't believe she knew I was there this morning.

"I saw you," she said.

"You saw me?"

"Yes I did," she said, "and I must say you'd better be a little sneakier this time around or you're going to get yourself into a heap of trouble."

"Alright," I said, "let me get this straight. You're on my side, right?"

"Yes," she said.

"And you think it's a good idea that I go down into the basement of the school to find out what Mrs. Tingledowner has been up to?"

"Yes," she said, looking more serious than ever, " and you'd better get going or you're going to run out of time. I've already done all that I can, or should do. You're on your own now, Coby."

With that she put the camera in my hand, pushed me out the door, and shut it in my face. I was alone now. I looked at the clock in the hallway. There was only fifteen minutes left in art class.

BELOW THE DOOR
IN THE FLOOR

By the time I got to the trap door in the floor I had thirteen minutes left before the kids would be heading back upstairs.

The hook was hanging in the same place it had been earlier. I was pretty sure that I would have to take the hook and put it into the hole in the door to open it. I did and it lifted surprisingly easy. After I lifted the door I put the hook back on the wall. Looking back on it now I realize how stupid that probably was. But I didn't want a Fleshbot to think that someone was down there.

I looked down into the opening in the floor and saw that there was a rope ladder dangling down to a cement floor below. I wasn't looking forward to this. I didn't even make it all the way down. I lost my grip and had to jump. I was fortunate enough to land on my back. It hurt like heck, but I'd managed to keep the camera safe.

It took me a moment to catch my breath and think straight. When I finally got my wits about me I looked up and realized I'd left the door in the floor open.

I placed the camera on the ground and up the ladder I went. I made it to the top and closed the door before falling back down after a step or two.

Once I finally caught my breath and stood up I was unable to see anything. It was pitch black! During my first fall, I'd noticed a light switch on the wall just behind the ladder. I flicked it on and was blinded by the bright fluorescent lights. When my eyes finally adjusted I couldn't believe what I saw.

There were passageways leading in every direction, each with any number of rope ladders leading up to who knows where. It was kind of weird though because the door in the floor was close to the end of the building, and yet several of the tunnels went past where the school would have ended.

To my right, just under where the music room would've been, there was a room with a refrigerator and a poster of some sort on the wall. I couldn't tell exactly what it said. I picked up the camera and took a few pictures of the ladder and the passageways leading in all directions. Then I headed to the room with the posters.

On one wall was a poster, completely black, except for two red dots about three inches apart from one another in the center. Above the dots it read:

We Are Superior
Us Above All Others

I snapped a picture of this and looked at the next poster. It had the picture of a boy, maybe a year or two older than me. He was standing in the hallway with his backpack, ready to go home. Above his head it read:

The Enemy
No Mercy Must Be Shown

Again, I snapped the picture before moving to the last poster in the room.

As soon as I looked at this poster I realized what it was, and I was sorry I'd come down here at all. For this was not a poster like the others. It was a map of the underground tunnels.

I took four pictures of the map at very close range.

I turned off the camera and headed back up to class. I climbed up the rope ladder. When I got to the top, the door in the floor wouldn't open. I tried not to panic. I searched the door for a latch that may have slid into place on the way down, but there was none.

I climbed back down the ladder and went over to the map. Had I been thinking clearly I'd have taken one of the passageways away from the school. Instead, I took the passage that led to Mrs. Giga's room.

I ran as fast as I could and must've climbed the correct ladder because I came out of the floor right under the second row of computers. Some boy named Peter Strauss was very surprised to see me. I was very surprised to see him as well - his being there meant Art class was over and my class would be upstairs.

"What on earth are you doing?" Mrs. Giga asked. The look on her face was a mixture of shock and amazement.

"Sorry to interrupt," I said. "I'm just returning the camera."

"He came right up here!" Peter was shouting. "He scared me! He came up right between my legs!"

"I'm sure he did Peter," said Mrs. Giga trying to calm the kindergartner down. She then turned to me and said, "Don't you think you need to say something to Peter, Coby?"

I told Peter I was sorry and handed her the camera. I told her it was very helpful and I got some good shots. She said she couldn't wait to see them.

With that I left and headed upstairs to my doom. I was sure that after this, I was going to have at least a month's worth of detention.

HER EYES

As I entered the classroom I could feel the stares of my classmates.

"Where have you been?" Mrs. Tingledowner bellowed from behind her desk.

I stood there in complete silence. I didn't know what to say.

"Well it doesn't matter much anyway," she said. "You and I will have plenty of time to chat about it. You can be sure of that."

Antoine came over to talk to me.

"Where were you?" he asked.

"I can't tell you," I said.

"Why not?" he asked.

"You had your chance to help," I said. I could feel my face start to burn.

"Alright," he said. "I was going to offer you my help, but if you don't want it that's fine."

I thought to myself for a minute.

"If you really want to help out I think I know a way you can do it," I said. He turned and started walking back toward me.

"Oh yeah," he said. "What's that?"

"You know Mrs. Giga?" I said.

"Yeah," he said.

65

"Well it just so happens that she has the same suspicions about Mr. Flannery and Mrs. Tingledowner as I do. At the end of the day," I whispered, "go down to Mrs. Giga. Tell her I sent you. Make sure she shows you what I gave her."

"What's that?" he asked.

"I can't tell you right now," I said looking around.

Tingledowner was on her way over to us.

"Just go to her tonight," I said.

"Are you two enjoying yourselves?" Mrs. Tingledowner asked. Then, without letting either one of us answer she shifted her gaze in my direction. "You and I will be enjoying ourselves shortly, won't we Coby?" With that she turned and walked away.

When I turned back to Antoine I could tell that he knew and understood everything. He was standing there with his jaw on the floor.

"Do you get it now?" I asked.

"Her eyes," was all he could muster. "Her eyes..."

DETENTION

After the last bus left and all of the other students had gone home, Mrs. Tingledowner walked over to my desk and stood over me.

"Why don't you tell me what you know?" she said.

There was no way I was going to tell her what I knew. Not until I was sure that Antoine had gotten to Mrs. Giga and they were on their way to save me.

"I asked you," she continued, "to tell me what you know."

"I'll never tell you!" I blurted out.

She put her hand on my arm. I started to pull away but she squeezed. It was harder than I'd ever been grabbed before. Her hand didn't feel like flesh. It felt like metal and it was crushing my arm.

"Stand up!" she commanded, her grip getting stronger.

I had no choice. I wasn't standing on my own. She was pulling me up. She dragged me across the classroom and shoved me hard into the hallway. I fell down against the wall.

"Get up!"

I rose as quickly as I could. I knew where we were headed and the way I looked at it, I could either go on my own, or I could go with my arm in her metallic grasp.

"It looks as though you know exactly where we're going," she said. "It's almost like you've been there before."

I slowed down and let her pass me. This was a mistake. She grabbed my other arm and began to drag me down the stairs.

"Do you take me for a fool?" she asked.

I couldn't respond. Her grip was too tight and I was trying to hold back my tears. I just had to wait a few more minutes. I knew Antoine and Mrs. Giga be down under the school waiting for us when we arrived and all would be well again.

*****

We were at the trap door in a matter of seconds.

"Open the door and get down there," Mrs. Tingledowner said.

I hesitated for just a moment. That was apparently too long for her. She grabbed me by the top of my head, giving me yet another thing in common with Suzy Trudell. In one motion the trap door opened and I was through the hole in a flash.

My hair – the hair that was left on my head – was still burning when I looked up and saw the hair that had come off in her hand floating ever so slowly toward me. It came to rest on the cement floor.

She finished clapping my hair off her hands and jumped down without using the rope ladder. She landed gracefully on her feet and turned toward me.

"Do you know where we are?" she asked as she walked by me and into the map room.

"Yes," I said. "It's your lair."

"Fool," she said.

She walked over to the map and pointed.

"Have you figured out what this is yet?" she asked pointing to the map. "Or do you need an explanation."

"It's a map of Marley," I said. "These tunnels lead to the homes of all the students."

"Bravo!" she exclaimed.

She put her finger to the map and pointed repeatedly.

"And do you know what this is underneath my finger?" she asked.

I knew, but I said nothing.

"This, Mr. Collins, is your house. Do you know, Mr. Collins, what we intend to do at your house?"

"No," I said.

She moved closer to me and her eyes lit up brighter than I'd ever seen. "We intend to make your life very difficult," she said. "That is, unless, you help us out."

"What do you want?" I asked.

"As Mr. Flannery and I were down here the other day, it occurred to us that the map is missing a few houses from the town," she said. "We thought it would be nice to know where those houses were and which kids lived in them - Just in case they get out of line."

"What does that have to do with me?" I asked.

"It's funny you should ask," she walked over to the couch and sat down. "Why don't you come over here and we can talk."

I picked myself up off the floor and walked over to the couch. She patted on the seat for me to sit down next to her. I did.

"Now," she said, "the only reason you're the one down here, and not your buddy Antoine, is that you mouthed off in class today. You're down here because you made a choice...a very poor choice."

She leaned forward and put her hand on my leg. I flinched a little, but to my surprise it didn't hurt. "If you've heard anything I've said in class this year," she continued, "you'll remember that choices have consequences, don't they?"

"Yes," I answered.

She had lulled me a little with her calmness. However, her sinister tone returned instantly. "I need you to point out some places on that map," she said.

"I'm not going to point out anything on that map," I said. "Not for you!"

"You stupid, stupid boy," she said. "You still haven't learned have you?" She rose from the couch and walked over to the rope ladder. "Send the other one down!" she yelled up.

In a matter of seconds the door opened and Antoine was thrust through the opening, his hair uneven and his arms bruised.

"You told me I could trust her," he said to me. "You told me she was on our side!"

"I thought she was," I told him. "How was I supposed to know that she wasn't who she said she was?"

Mrs. Giga came down the ladder, her head flipped back so that only her robotic head was visible. She threw Antoine onto the couch next to me.

"Now," Mrs. Giga said, "where do we begin?" I stared at her in disbelief. She had tricked me so easily. "I know what you're thinking," she said. "You want to know how I was able to fool you so easily. It was simple, Coby. You are a very stupid boy."

"How did you know?" I asked Antoine.

"It was easy," he said. "Look at her nails."

I looked. They were not smooth like normal nails. They had small screws that were barely visible sticking out of them, like they'd been attached; like they were part of a machine. I should have seen these when she handed me the camera.

"I'm sorry," I said. "I should have paid more attention to you guys at lunch."

"Well it's a little late now," he said.

Mrs. Tingledowner walked over to the map again. "Alright you two," she began. "I need some information and I'm getting really tired of waiting. So if one of you could please come over here and point out where Toby Bickell lives, that would be most helpful."

"We're not doing that!" said Antoine.

"You know Devindra," said Mrs. Giga pointing at Antoine, "I knew that one would be trouble when he came to me. He's not nearly as helpless as the fat one."

There was a moment of silence before footsteps could be heard getting closer to the trap door. Mr. Flannery was coming down to join us.

*****

"Do you know anything that can get us out of this?" I asked Antoine while the other two filled Flannery in on the situation.

"There's one thing," he said. "Fleshbots are very competitive. If we could find a way to get them to argue with each other we might be able to buy enough time to get most of the way to your house before they've realized what's happened."

"Okay," I said. "How do we do that?" Before Antoine could say anything they were on us again.

"Boys," Mr. Flannery said. "It appears to me that you have been very disrespectful to my two favorite teachers."

"They're refusing to show us the Bickell house on the map!" said Mrs. Tingledowner.

Mrs. Giga looked confused and so did Mr. Flannery.

"Devindra," Mr. Flannery asked, "why are you looking for Toby Bickell's house?"

"I can explain," Mrs. Tingledowner stammered. "He needs to be punished."

"He needs to be punished?" Mrs. Giga asked, turning toward Mr. Flannery with a quizzical look. "We agreed that no one younger that seven was to be targeted! Toby's only in kindergarten! Are you going to allow this?"

"I will allow nothing of the sort," Mr. Flannery replied in a sharp tone.

"But..." Mrs. Tingledowner had turned to make her point and the three were instantly engulfed in argument.

Antoine nudged me and tilted his head toward the corridor that led in the direction of my house. We started to run in that direction. We hadn't gotten as far as we'd hoped when they came to their senses.

"They're getting away!" we heard Tingledowner scream.

Within seconds they were chasing us. It was dark and I was running out of breath fast. Antoine was well ahead of me.

"Do you know where my house is?" I yelled.

"I'm hoping it's up there somewhere," he said pointing down the corridor. "The closer the better!"

I couldn't have agreed with him more. I was really getting tired.

"Do you see that?" I panted.

"Yeah," Antione said. "It looks like a ladder!" He was going to get there much sooner than I was. I saw him get to the ladder and climb up. Then he was gone and I was still running. I didn't even have a chance to get a foot on the ladder before Flannery had a hold of me.

"Nice try fat boy," he said. "But not nice enough."

"What are you going to do to me?" I asked.

"Let's see," he said. "You've broken our trust. We're going to have to make you one of us now." A smile came over his face. "But just to show you that we're good sports about it, we're going to give you the chance to get into your house. With any luck we can get your sister too. She's the smart one!"

I should've been scared out of my mind, but to tell you the truth, I wasn't. Antoine had been up there for almost two full minutes. By now he must've come up with something.

"Go ahead, boy!" Flannery said. "Climb!"

I did as he said. They gave me a head start and allowed me to climb up into the downstairs bathroom of my house. As I got to the top of the ladder I saw Antoine. He put his finger to his lips and waited for me to get out of the hole.

The hole was located just under the edge of the toilet. Antoine was ready. He had stuffed five full rolls of toilet paper into the bowl.

"What are you doing?" I asked. "My parents are going to kill us."

"Really?" he asked. He looked down at the three teachers. "We'll deal with your parents later."

The three of them were already on their way up the ladder. Antoine began flushing frantically.

"They're robots Coby," he said. "What do robots hate more than anything?"

"Water!" I said. "Why didn't I think of that?"

I suddenly realized that Suzy Trudell knew what the other kids didn't. If she could get enough water on the bathroom floor she'd be safe. But somebody had turned her in before she could do it.

Flannery, Tingledowner, and Giga continued to climb, as did the water level in the toilet. It wasn't yet to the top when Flannery emerged.

"We've got you now!" he said, just as the water dropped onto his face.

His hand was around my ankle, but he quickly let go as more and more water rushed over the edge of the bowl. Sparks began to fly from his face, as they did from the faces of the other two robots below. They fell from the ladder down to the ground.

They were on the cement next to each other, squirming and trying to get out of the water's way. But the damage had been done. They started to move slower and slower until finally they failed to move.

It was over.

"I owe you big time Antoine," I said. "Big time!"

"Yup," he said, "You do."

EPILOGUE

As you can imagine my parents were not happy when they got home. They did say that the mess was much better than the alternative.

When news of the Fleshbot teachers broke, many of the parents began to pull their kids out of our school and move to neighboring towns, where they were sure there would be no more Fleshbot teachers.

After a few weeks though, many of the schools had reported cases similar to ours.

All the remaining teachers at Marley passed a water exposure test. Tingledowner, Giga, and Flannery had been the only Fleshbots. We were pretty lucky compared to some of the other schools. Because of this my parents and Antoine's parents agreed to let us continue going to Marley Elementary.

Antoine and I were happy when the year came to an end. It would be a great summer. The best part was we were both going to be in Mrs. Rutlidge's class for fourth grade.

Let the adventures continue!

COBY COLLINS
AND THE
HEXBOLT
OF DOOM

MARLEY ELEMENTARY
ADVENTURES
VOLUME TWO

JUSTIN
JOHNSON

Contents

PROLOGUE

"RUN!"

I looked around, trying to figure out which way would be best. Should I go in the direction of my friend Antoine, who was shackled to the wall? He needed my help desperately, and if I made the choice to leave him I would surely never see him again.

Should I go in the direction of the hex bolt? The very hex bolt that put us in this position in the first place; the hex bolt that, if we'd never seen it, or simply decided to leave it on the ground would be covered in cement and lost forever.

Should I run in the direction of Tingledowner, Flannery and Giga? They had shackled Antoine to the wall and were now looking to do the same to me.

"Yes, Coby, RUN!" Tingledowner said, mocking Antoine's plea. "Run as fast as you can, fatty. We'll catch you anyway. We know where you live remember?"

I remembered all too well that they knew where I lived. Last year they had followed me to my house. Antoine and I destroyed them with toilet water. Yet, here we were in this same predicament again. Only this time I have to make the choice to either save myself or save my friend.

"You better do something, boy, or your family's going to wonder what happened to you?" Flannery said as he walked in my direction.

I looked around again. It was hot down here, and dark. We were surrounded by rock in a circular shaped room. It was what I'd imagined the inside of a volcano would look like. The only ways out was the door Antoine was chained to or the hex bolt.

I was surrounded. Tingledowner was coming from my left, Flannery was coming from behind me, and Giga was coming from my right. I had to make a decision quickly.

"Coby," Antoine yelled. "Go get Suzy!"

Antoine was right. I had to get Suzy, but could I really leave him down here? How would I live with myself?

Tingledowner got to me first. I felt her finger on my wrist and I moved quickly away from her before she could close her grasp. I made my move. There was only one choice to make.

RAISIN BRAN BANANA

I started to run toward the hex bolt. Antoine would be fine. He knew the best way to handle Fleshbots, so I had to listen to him. There was no turning back now. They were right behind me and I could feel them closing in.

I was almost there. I could see the hex bolt in the distance.

"Get him!" Giga yelled from behind Tingledowner and Flannery. "He's getting away!"

She was right. I was getting away. I was so close now, just a few more steps. I reached out and grabbed the hex bolt.

I had it in my hand. Suddenly, I felt a strange feeling come over me. It felt like I was falling.

"Look at you, you big spaz!"

What?

I could hear a voice. It didn't sound like any of the voices down in the volcano. I was beginning to fall faster now – faster than I'd ever fallen. I couldn't see the ground below. When would this stop? I closed my eyes and curled up.

"Come on dork! We're going to be late. It's the first day of school and I'm for sure going to get perfect attendance this year!"

I awoke to see my sister Jill walking out of my bedroom. As she left she grabbed the end of my sheets and pulled them off of me. I could smell a faint hint of her breakfast. Thankfully, we didn't have any green onion cream cheese in the house. This morning she must've settled for a bowl of Raisin Bran and a banana. You know, it's not such a bad smell.

I finally managed to peel myself out of bed. I was covered in sweat. This had become a common occurrence since last year. I found that I was having nightmares almost every night, and I would often times be drenched in the morning.

I staggered into the bathroom to clean myself up before putting my clothes on for school. As I was splashing water on my face I heard the familiar hissing sound of the bus brakes. I rushed to my room and looked out the window just in time to see my sister get on the bus. I waited for just a second to see if the bus was going to stay and wait for me. It did not. My sister was barely up the third step and the doors swung shut. The bus lurched forward and was gone.

I returned to the bathroom to finish washing my face. My mom was standing in the doorway with her arms crossed. She looked upset.

"Coby, you need to hurry up," she said.

"I know."

"I have a meeting in twenty minutes and now I have to take you to school too." She walked away from the bathroom and went down stairs.

I finished brushing my teeth, put on a white T-shirt and Khaki shorts, grabbed my bag and headed to the kitchen.

"Do I have time to get breakfast?" I asked.

My mom handed me a banana.

I looked at the banana and then at my stomach. "Do you really think this'll be enough?"

My mom muttered something under her breath - I'm pretty sure it was a good thing I didn't hear what it was – and handed me another banana.

"Now go get in the car!"

*****

The ride to school was quiet and quick. Mom drove faster than usual and didn't say a word until we got into the parking lot.

"Honey," she said, "You had another nightmare didn't you?"

"Yes."

"Do you want to tell me about it?" she asked.

"No."

She had a disappointed look on her face. She'd been asking me this same question every morning for months. And every morning I'd told her that I didn't want to talk about it.

"Coby, I understand if you don't want to talk about it," she said. "But, at some point, you're going

87

to have to do something to move past this. You can't go on having nightmares all your life."

She was right. I knew it. But how could I possibly forget what I'd seen last year? How could I possibly forget the red eyes of Tingledowner or the sweat smell that emanated from Flannery's office, or being duped by Giga?

"Alright mom," I said, "I'll try my best."

With that she leaned over and gave me a kiss on the cheek. I pulled away just a little because there were kids walking past our car and into the school. I liked that my mother wanted to give me a kiss, but I was in fourth grade now. I couldn't let anybody see me receiving a kiss from my mom.

CLOSING THE DOOR IN THE FLOOR

I had just settled into my seat when an announcement came over the speaker in our classroom.

"Attention everybody, sorry to interrupt. This is Principal Shelman and I would like to call an assembly in the auditorium. Please have all of your students there in thirty minutes."

Mrs. Rutlidge, our new teacher, looked annoyed.

I looked at Antoine, "What do you think Mr. Shelman is going to tell us?"

"I don't know," he said.

*****

As we arrived at the auditorium it felt like something very exciting was happening. It was the first day of school, and as long as I'd been going to Marley, there'd never been an assembly on the first day, for any reason.

I looked around and saw my sister, Jill. She stuck her tongue out at me and made an L with her left index finger and thumb on her forehead. I smiled and gave her a wave.

We walked past several rows of seats and finally settled on a row near the middle of the auditorium. I sat down next to Antoine and began to look around. All the kids seemed to be in a fervor this morning. It was apparent that nobody knew what this was about.

I took one quick glance toward the back rows and saw Suzy Trudell had just reached her seat. She looked at me and I turned away very quickly. I didn't want to stare, or make her feel like I was looking at her. She'd been through quite an ordeal last year with Flannery. I'm sure she already had a lot of people staring at her.

The lights flickered and Mr. Shelman walked out. He walked slowly to the center of the stage, looking intensely at the gathered crowd.

"Good Morning," he said. The microphone boomed and a small ring of feedback made everyone cringe a little. "I'm sure you're all wondering why we're here, in the auditorium, instead of in our classrooms."

Everyone in the auditorium nodded.

"Well," he continued, "some of you will remember that we had quite an end to last year."

Antoine put his hand on his wrist to rub his faded bruises. I felt my hair. Even though it had grown back in, the burn that I felt when Tingledowner chopped it off had not gone away. It wasn't there all the time, but when something reminded me of last year I could feel it flare up. I turned to look at Suzy again. She was trying not to cry, but it was no use. Her eyes were bloodshot and glassy looking. A few tears started to fall down her cheeks before she hid her face in her hands. I turned back to Mr. Shelman.

"As a result, we have a number of things we have to do to make our school a safer place for all of our students. We want to ensure that nothing like that ever happens again," he said. "Many of the steps we are taking do not concern you at this point, and many of them have already been done. We've installed new locks on the doors, and a security scan for any teacher or parent wishing to enter the building."

I could see all of the teachers nodding their heads in agreement.

"Finally," he said, "I am getting to the part that requires your help." A number of students sat right up, their ears perked. "The Fleshbots constructed an elaborate tunnel system underneath our school. These tunnels were used to connect our school to your houses. Unfortunately, it didn't end there. They were also used to connect our neighborhood to other neighborhoods, and our school to other schools. It seems that these things...these, Fleshbots, have taken up residence all over the country. We may not be able to stop them in every location, but we will do our best to stop them from invading Marley ever again!"

The audience erupted into huge cheers. Teacher and students, alike, gave each other satisfied smiles and high fives. Mr. Shelman waited a few long seconds, clearly enjoying the applause, before he continued.

"In order to do this, we must fill in the tunnels. Our school and our great town of Marley, along with the other schools and other towns have decided to work together to accomplish this task. As for the part that involves you - we need several of our older students to help clean out the tunnels before the construction crews can come in and finish the job. There will be a sign up sheet in every room for grades four through six. Any student wishing to take on the job must sign up by the end of the week."

Excitement filled the room. Everybody was talking about how they were going to sign up.

I looked at Antoine. He was shaking his head. "No way," he said. "I'm never going back there again - Absolutely not!"

"Agreed," I said.

I took a quick look back to see what Suzy's reaction was.

She was gone.

GET TO WORK

We had only been back in the classroom for about five minutes when Mrs. Rutlidge called Antoine and I back to her desk.

"Antoine, Coby...I'm sorry I haven't much of a chance to introduce myself this morning. I'm Mrs. Rutlidge."

"We know," Antoine said.

"I was speaking with Principal Shelman yesterday and he had mentioned that you two had a big part to play in saving Marley last year."

Antoine and I looked at each other. We weren't quite sure what she was getting at and it was making us both a little uncomfortable. We didn't really feel like we'd saved anything - except ourselves.

"Okay?" Antoine said.

"Well," Mrs. Rutlidge said, "Mr. Shelman and I thought it would be a great idea for you two to lead the cleanup efforts down in the tunnels. With your experience, we both feel that you'd be able to do a great job!"

"No way," said Antoine. "I'm never going back down there again."

"Me, either," I said.

"Boys, don't be so hasty," Mrs. Rutlidge said. "You have until Friday to think about it. Take some time and let me know."

*****

"No way!" Antoine yelled as we left school. "No way, am I going back down there! Absolutely not!"

He was walking really fast and I was having a difficult time trying to keep up. A few of the older kids were laughing at me because I was breathing heavy and trying to pull my pants up.

"Antoine," I said, "could you slow down, please?"

Antoine finally slowed down as we approached the bus line. I stopped to put my hands on my knees and hunch over.

"I was thinking," I said, "it might not be a bad idea to help out with the clean-up."

"Are you insane?!"

"Maybe a little," I said. "But think about it. My mother's been telling me all summer that I would have to do something to get past the nightmares I've been having. Maybe this is it."

He gave me a look that said 'I don't believe you.' And then he turned and walked toward his bus. I chased.

"Seriously," I said. "It might be just what the doctor ordered, to go down there and help destroy that place."

"I don't think so, Coby. No way, not me."

"You owe me!" I said.

"No I don't! What're you talking about?" he said. "If anybody owes anybody, you owe me!"

He was right. I did owe him, but I thought I might be able to get one over on him. I was desperate. I'd somehow convinced myself that I needed to do this, but I wasn't going to do it without Antoine. I had to go for it. I had to throw my last ditch effort at him - the guilt trip.

"But Antoine," I started, getting a little pouty, "who am I gonna have down there that can help me the way you can?"

"Knock it off, Coby."

"No, seriously," I continued, laying it on really thick, "you've always been there for me. Anytime I needed something, it was Antoine. Anytime I had any free time at all, it was Antoine. And now, I want to help clean the tunnel system and...no Antoine." As I finished this last part I really let my bottom lip hang out and I made puppy dog eyes, just for a little extra oomph.

Antoine looked around. Some of the other kids were watching the whole scene and he knew that if he didn't agree, I'd just keep going. That's one thing Antoine hates more than Fleshbots - being seen with me when I'm making the pouty face.

"I don't understand why you want to do this so bad," he said.

"Neither do I, but I feel like I need to."

"Oh, alright," he finally agreed. "But after this, we are finished with Fleshbot stuff, promise."

"I promise," I said.

*****

The work began on the Monday following sign ups. There were a lot of kids who showed up the first day to see what all the fuss was about, but when they found out how much work would be involved, they quickly found other things to do.

"I can't believe I let you talk me in to this," Antoine said as he picked up a box and started walking it toward the construction man in charge.

"Quiet," the man said. "Enough talking you two, more work."

It was day three and there wasn't very much left to pick up. There weren't very many of us left to pick it up, either. Aside from Antoine and me, there were only four other kids. There was Simon Dinkledge, John Sufril, Kathy Woderkows, and Leslie Vitriol. Antoine and I weren't sure exactly what they were doing there.

They certainly weren't a lot of help. They moved slowly, didn't lift much, and basically just seemed like they were there to say 'we were there!' Antoine and I had done most of the heavy lifting and now we were near the end of it.

There was just one thing left to move...the couch. The same couch that Antoine and I had had to sit on last year while Tingledowner asked us to point out Toby Bickell's house; The same couch, upon which I had had a very strange talk with Mrs. Tingledowner about choices; The very couch that Antoine had been thrown onto after discovering that Mrs. Giga was not, in fact, on our side. This was the couch - The final thing that connected us to them.

"What do you say?" I said to Antoine, nodding toward the couch.

"Let's get rid of her," he said.

As we approached the ends of the couch, the construction man said, "You two! Get away from that thing, you'll hurt yourselves!"

He turned over his shoulder and yelled up the ladder to another construction man. "Ernie," he said. "Come on down here. We got these two little kids trying to lift this giant couch."

Ernie came down the ladder and positioned himself at one end of the couch. The other construction man didn't move. "You gonna help me with this, Jim?" Ernie finally said.

"Yeah," said Jim, clearly amused by himself. "I was just wondering how long it was gonna take ya before ya noticed." He chuckled a little bit and then positioned himself for the lift.

The two men picked up the couch and began to move it. As they did, I noticed something out of the corner of my eye. It was on the floor against the wall and it gave a slight twinkle as the fluorescent light shone on it.

"Do you see that?" Antoine asked.

"Yeah, I see it," I said.

"What is it?"

"I don't think I want to know," I said.

HEX BOLT

I walked over to the shiny piece of metal that lay on the floor behind where the couch had just been. It appeared to be some kind of bolt.

"What is it?" I asked Antoine.

"It looks like a hex bolt," he said.

"What's that?" I asked.

He looked at me like I was a half-wit. He explained to me that it was a bolt and the top part, the part that you use to screw it into things, had six sides.

"Oh," I said, "like a hexagon has six sides!"

"Congratulations," he said, "you're a genius."

We both stood there staring at it for a few moments. Neither one of us knew what to do with it.

"I'm going to pick it up," I said.

Antoine looked at me, his eyebrows furled, "I don't think that's such a great idea Coby."

I should have listened to him, but I didn't. I reached down and picked up the hex bolt and then Antoine was gone. And so were the tunnels and the posters. Everything was gone.

*****

I woke up laying a dirt floor. I looked around and saw that I was inside what seemed to be a hollowed out volcano, except the top, where the hole would normally be, was closed in. It was dark down here, but not pitch black. I could see a little.

The hex bolt was no longer in my hands. I must've dropped it when I hit the ground. It had come to rest about thirty feet away from where I was sitting. I should have just picked it up and tried to return to the school, but I was curious.

I started to walk around. Everything looked closed in and dusty. There was one door on the opposite wall from where I was standing. It was large and green. It was made of metal and had bolts all around the edge. I walked toward it.

I reached out my hand and opened it. As I did this I closed my eyes in case I didn't like what was on the other side.

I waited ten full seconds before I opened them. What I saw was enough to give me nightmares forever.

There were glass like tubes, each the size of a grown man or woman. Inside the tubes were people. They were just lying there, and there were rubber hoses running into the top and bottom of each chamber. It looked like there was some sort of air or gas being pumped into them.

As I began examining the tubes I noticed that every single person inside them had some sort of soot or black powder around their forehead. Upon closer look I began to notice little screws in their finger nails.

These were not people – they were FLESHBOTS!

I had to get out of there – and fast! As I turned to run back toward the door I saw the three chambers against the wall on the side of the room where I'd come in. Inside of these was something that made my blood run cold. For now it became apparent what this place was. This was a Fleshbot repair shop. Inside the chambers against the wall lay the bodies of Tingledowner, Flannery, and Giga.

I ran past the door trying not to look at the still bodies of our three foes from a year ago. I ran right to the hex bolt. As I bent over to pick it up I thought I heard Tingledowner's voice. It said, "We're going to get you Coby!"

With that, I grabbed the hex bolt and was gone.

GOTTA TALK TO SUZY

I landed on the floor of the tunnels with a thud. I could hear a great deal of commotion. There were flashlights in the distance and someone yelling, "He's over here!"

A police man and several other grown-ups, including my parents came rushing toward me.

"Coby," my mom yelled, "where have you been? You've had the whole town worried sick?"

"Yes Coby," my father followed, "tell us where you've been."

How long had I been down there? It had seemed to me like a matter of minutes, but there was no way all of these people could be searching like this if I'd only been gone for a few minutes.

"Antoine and I, found a hex bolt on the floor," I started.

Everyone was silent now. Their eyes were focused on me.

"He told me not to pick it up, but I did anyway," I said. "When I picked it up, it took me away from here. I'm not sure where, exactly, but someplace different. It was dark and cold and looked like the inside of a volcano."

My parents were starting to shake their heads. They didn't believe me. Why should they? I was sounding crazy. I decided to stop talking and give up. I ran to my mother, sobbing and gave her a hug around her waist. My father put his hand on my head.

"Let's go home, son," my father said. "Sorry about the trouble everyone, thank you for all of your help."

Then my parents took me home.

*****

When I saw Antoine the next day he looked exhausted. He embraced me because he was so happy that I was still alive, and then he pushed me into a locker because I hadn't listened to him about the hex bolt.

He told me that he didn't get much sleep the night before. He told me that he spent the entire night worrying about me. This was made worse for him after the search party formed. They wouldn't let him help. They called his mother and had her pick him up.

"Do you want to know what I saw?" I asked.

"No," he responded sharply.

"Look, I'm sorry I picked up the hex bolt and disappeared," I said, "but we've got bigger problems now."

"What's this we stuff?" he said. "I didn't even want to go down and clean up those tunnels – that was you."

"I know, but - "

"And," he interrupted, "I told you not to touch that hex bolt."

"Yeah, I know, but - "

"I'm not interested, Coby. I'm sorry, I'm just not. I want to move on and forget about last year. I don't ever want to think about another Fleshbot again!"

"You don't understand," I said, "they still exist. We didn't kill them; they're alive in these chamber things. I saw them. I saw Tingledowner and Flannery and Giga and they are still alive!"

He stopped dead in his tracks.

"I have to go back," I said.

"No, you don't!"

"Yes, I do," I said, "and I need your help."

He put his head down and stared at the floor. I knew he didn't want anything to do with this, and quite frankly, neither did I. But if we didn't do something, what would happen?

Finally he looked at me and said, "Alright. I'll do it. But we won't be able to defeat them alone."

"I was thinking about that, too," I said. "I have an idea."

"What?"

"We've gotta talk to Suzy Trudell."

SUZY TRUDELL

I made it through the entire morning and didn't remember a single word that Mrs. Rutlidge said. All I could think about was Tingledowner coming back to serve me up one last detention. I was also trying to figure out a way to talk to Suzy Trudell.

It was weird. We'd never even spoken before and now I was going to try to ask her if she would help Antoine and me go to this place in who knows where and defeat Fleshbots that we all thought were dead. I didn't have a great deal of faith in this working, but I had to give it a shot.

I usually saw Suzy at the end of my lunch period. As we were leaving the cafeteria her class was just coming in to start their lunch.

"Mrs. Rutlidge?" I asked as we were lining up and getting ready to head back to our classroom for the afternoon.

"Yes, Coby," she said.

"May I use the bathroom?"

"Can you wait until we get upstairs?" she asked. Why is it teachers can never let you just go to the bathroom when you say you have to go? It's like they want to make you wait a little, just to be sure you're telling the truth. For cases like this you have to bring out the old 'poopy doopy.'

"No, I have to go poop," I said. I even added a little pee pee dance to add to the authenticity.

She rolled her eyes a little, but she knew that the inconvenience of me getting back to the room late was far better than the inconvenience of me soiling myself. "Go ahead."

The rest of my class headed upstairs and I headed toward the bathroom. When I was sure they were gone I headed back into the cafeteria to talk to Suzy.

*****

She sat alone. She ate with her head down, like she didn't want to be bothered. I walked over to her table and took a seat directly across from her. She looked up and her eyes met mine. Her eyes were hard and joyless. She seemed to be staring right through me, like she didn't see me. I'm sure she wished I was invisible. Then she put her head back down and continued eating her lunch.

"Um," I started nervously, "hi, Suzy."

She didn't answer. She just kept eating.

"My name is Coby Collins."

Nothing.

"I had an experience very similar to yours last year."

She took a drink of her water and a quick bite of her grilled cheese sandwich.

"I can see you're busy and I don't want to bother you. I'm just going to leave this right here," I said.

I pulled out a sheet of paper that I'd prepared in case I got this particular response. The message on the paper read as follows:

Suzy,

I know you probably don't want to talk.

Please reconsider and meet Antoine and

me at 4:00

this afternoon at the playground.

-Coby

I put the paper down on the table and walked away. When I got to the cafeteria door I looked back - just once. The paper was gone.

*****

Antoine looked at his watch. "It's 4:05 man. She's not gonna show."

I had a feeling this was probably true, but I wanted to give her just a little more time. She was the only other student at Marley Elementary who knew what Antoine and I were going through. She was the only other person who could possibly help us.

"Just give her a few more minutes," I said. "If she doesn't show up, I'll try again tomorrow. But I think we need to give her some time to think about this."

"If she's smart, she'll stay away," Antoine said, picking up a stone and throwing it up a slide. "I know I would if wasn't friends with you."

He was right. This was crazy. What were we doing? Sitting on a playground waiting for a girl who wanted nothing to do with anyone, let alone us. We didn't even want to do what we were doing.

Antoine went over to the bench and sat down. He checked his watch again.

"Just give it time, Antoine."

"So," he said, "how are you going to convince her to join our team of Fleshbot killing, vigilante fourth graders, anyway?"

I hadn't thought of this. I didn't know what I would say if she were to show up. I guess I hadn't really counted on her showing up.

"I don't know. I guess I would tell her that we were a lot alike and then probably discuss the whole hex bolt thing."

"Yeah...go on," Antoine said. He was now whittling a stick with a pocketknife his parents had gotten him over the summer if he'd promised to leave them alone.

"I don't know. I'd probably just ask her to help us - plain and simple."

"No," a voice said from behind a tree.

Antoine and I looked at each other and then in the direction of the tree. Antoine rose from the bench and walked with me over to the big maple tree that loomed over the playground.

Behind the maple tree, sitting with her knees tucked under her chin was Suzy Trudell.

NO WAY

Antoine and I stood at the edge of the playground staring down at Suzy Trudell. She had tucked herself into a little ball. She'd been sitting there the entire time and had heard everything Antoine and I had said.

"Hi," I said, finally breaking the silence.

"Hello," she said in return.

I reached out my hand to her. "I'm Coby."

She shook my hand and said, "I know, we met this afternoon."

"This is Antoine," I said pointing to Antoine. "He was down there with me last year."

"I know," she said, "word travels fast in Marley."

"Yeah," I agreed.

The three of us stayed there, in awkward silence, for several minutes before Suzy said, "Well, it was nice to meet you two. I have to go home now."

She stood up and started to walk away when Antoine said, "Wait. Why won't you do it?"

Suzy stopped and without facing us said, "Because I'm like you Antoine. I just want to move on."

"You won't be able to," said Antoine.

"Watch me."

"Antoine's right," I said. "There is no moving on...not until these things are destroyed. They're still alive and they are going to come back to finish what they started."

"How do you know they're still alive?" she asked, and then in a mocking tone said, "Do you see them in your dreams?"

"No," I said, a little louder than I wanted to. "I saw them yesterday and I know how to get back to them. That's why we're here talking to you. Because for some reason they wanted you, too. Now, doesn't that make you want to finish what we started last year?"

"What who started?" she asked. "You started this Coby. I had no intention of defeating them. I was playing their game and going along with them. You're the one that stood up; you're the one who fought."

The more I thought about it, the more I realized she was right. It was me. I was the one who fought back. Not Antoine, until he had to. And not Suzy. She had taken their punishments and cowered to them.

"What do you mean you played their game?" Antoine asked.

"I played their game," she said. "I did what they told me to do and I took whatever punishment Flannery wanted to give me. I thought that if I went along with everything they'd just go away and leave me alone."

She turned to face us now. Tears were welling in her eyes. "I used to be a good girl," she said. "I still am a good girl, but nobody believes that anymore."

Antoine and I stood there, speechless. We had treated this girl like a mystery for the last year, wondering what she was all about. And now we were going to find out.

"I used to be a little princess," she said. "I wore dresses and read books and played with my friends. And then Flannery took a liking to me. I was in third grade, just like you were. He came up into the classroom and asked Mrs. Tingledowner who the smartest student in the class was. She told him I was."

Suzy bent over and picked a weed. She started tearing it apart in her hand as she continued. "He took me down to his office and told me he had a very important job, and that I was the only one in the school who could do it. I had to give him names of any third grader in the building who I thought was trustworthy.

"For a few months I gave him the names of my friends. I thought that he was going to give them special awards or something. I didn't know that he was going to try to recruit them as Fleshbots. He started putting them through the most horrible tests to see if they were worthy.

"By the time I realized what was going on none of my friends were speaking with me anymore. They knew it was I who'd turned them in. And they thought I knew Flannery's intentions.

"I went to Flannery and told him I didn't want to play his game anymore. I told him he could find someone else. From that moment he made me a target. He would barge into our classroom and take me to his office for punishment. He would make a big deal about what I'd done in front of everyone so they would think I was a trouble maker. All of the things he said were lies.

"The only one that really happened was the toilet plugging last year. That was self-defense. I'd escaped his office and he chased me into the bathroom. I tried to get enough water between myself and him, but obviously I'd failed.

"I was so relieved when I heard what you two had done. But it didn't last long, because Flannery had already ruined my life. He took away all my friends and isolated me from everyone else.

"And now you two come to me and ask me if I want another shot at getting even with Flannery? My answer is no. No way. Not now, not ever. Please leave me alone, like the other kids, and don't talk to me anymore."

She turned and left. Neither Antoine, nor I called out to her. We just let her go. What else were we going to do?

THE DREAM

When I got home that night I was greatly troubled. Suzy Trudell was nothing like I thought she would be. She had been one of our school's best students and Flannery had destroyed her. I had a very difficult time getting to sleep. I lay on my pillow for hours thinking over and over about her story and how her life had been ruined. I finally drifted to sleep.

I had a dream that we were down in the volcano. Antoine was shackled to the door and the Fleshbots were chasing me. But this time there was someone different, someone I'd never met. It was a little girl. She was tied with rope at her hands and feet. She was unconscious on the floor. She couldn't have been any older than five or six. "Coby," Antoine yelled, "go get Suzy!"

I stood there trying to put the pieces together, but I couldn't. Who was this girl? Where had she come from? And how could I leave her and Antoine down there alone to go get Suzy?

*****

My sister woke me up as usual by ripping the covers off and breathing in my face as she shouted at me. My mother had gotten groceries this week and green onion cream cheese must've been on the list. Jill's breath was horrible!

I had to rush to clean up and get ready for the bus. As usual I was covered in sweat. The bus had started to leave our house when I came running up the driveway. It was a few feet up the road when it finally stopped. As I scaled the steps Mr. Turley looked at me and said, "One more time and I'm gonna leave ya!"

The other kids on the bus took turns snickering at me as I got to my seat. Antoine was already there looking out the window.

"Good morning," I said.

"Morning," he returned.

I knew he was kind of over the whole Fleshbot thing, so I wasn't really sure if I should tell him about my dream. I decided it wouldn't be the best way to start the day. We sat there in silence until Suzy got on the bus.

"Who's that?" I asked pointing out the window. Suzy wasn't alone this morning. I recognized the little girl that was next to her from my dream.

"That's Suzy," Antoine said, "and her sister."

"She has a sister?" I asked.

"Yeah, maybe if you woke up on time to ride the bus a little more, you'd know who she was."

Suzy was holding her sister's hand as they came up the steps. She didn't let go until they were in their seats. Suzy looked tired. She looked frazzled, like she'd woken up late and hadn't had time to run a brush through her hair or wash her face.

"She looks awful," I said to Antoine.

"She does," he agreed.

When we arrived at school and we were all let off the bus, Suzy waited at the bottom of the steps with her sister. As soon as Antoine and I reached the bottom she stopped us.

"I need to talk with you two...later." She walked away, holding her sister's hand tighter than she had when they got onto the bus.

"What do you think she wants to talk about?" Antoine asked me.

"I don't know," I said.

*****

Another morning went by and I had no idea what Mrs. Rutlidge had taught us. All I could think about was getting to the end of lunch so I could talk to Suzy and find out what she had on her mind.

"I can't imagine what it could be," I said to Antoine during our mid-morning break. "Do you think she's changed her mind?"

"I doubt it," he said. "She doesn't want anything to do with this, Coby."

"I know," I said. "But that's what she said yesterday. Remember, you didn't want to help clean up the tunnels."

"Yeah, and I was right. We should've stayed out of there."

"I agree," I said. "But my point is this – you changed your mind. It's possible that, after a night to think about it, she may have come to a different conclusion."

"I think you're nuts," Antoine said as he walked back to his seat. Break time was over.

In an hour I'd see Suzy at lunch.

*****

I was pretty hungry. I wolfed down my food in the first five minutes. It may have been the anticipation of seeing what Suzy had on her mind. Sometimes when I get excited I eat too fast. Whatever it was I had a long time to sit there and wait.

I felt like I was in one of those movies where they go between the clock and the kid. The kid's just waiting for the end of the school day, or whatever. And the clock is like one minute away from the bell ringing. And then all the kid hears is tick, tock, tick, tock. Well that was me - except I had twenty five minutes.

Finally it was time to dump our trays and line up. There was no way I was going to use the poop excuse two days in a row. Mrs. Rutlidge would get suspicious, and then there'd be phone calls home and trips to the doctor and all that stuff that grownups do when they get worried.

I'd spent all morning thinking about this moment, but I hadn't actually thought about how to get to the other side of the cafeteria to talk to Suzy.

I didn't have to.

"Ms. Trudell! Get back here right now!" Mrs. Poley was yelling at Suzy, who was crossing the cafeteria. She was walking toward me and didn't seem to notice that she was being called elsewhere.

She walked right up to me and handed me a folded up scrap of paper. She moved her face close to mine and whispered in my ear. "Do what this says."

"Okay," I said.

She turned and walked back toward her seat and a very angry Mrs. Poley. My class headed up stairs for our afternoon lessons.

SUZY'S DREAM

The Maple — 4:00

~Suzy

That was all the note said. Great, I thought, now I've gotta wait until after school to find out what's going on. It was infuriating. All this suspense was killing me.

As I expected, the afternoon dragged and dragged and dragged. Finally, the kid staring at the clock and listening to the tick and tock was released by the bell.

Antoine and I ran out to the maple tree. Well, Antoine ran...and I did what I could. We both arrived at the tree out of breath.

Suzy was not alone. She had the little girl who'd gotten on the bus with her this morning. "I want you guys to meet my sister, Jenny," she said. Then turning to her sister said, "Jenny this is Coby and his friend, Antoine. They were the ones I was telling you about. They're going to help us."

"Nice to meet you," I said to Jenny. What did Suzy and her sister need help with? Yesterday Suzy was perfectly fine letting everything go and now, all of the sudden she wanted our help.

I gave Antoine a look and shrugged my shoulders. He shrugged his shoulders back. Suzy crouched down to talk to her sister at eye level and told her to play on the playground until she was finished talking with us.

"I had a dream last night," she began, "a really bad dream."

"Me too," I said. "Your sister was in mine."

Suzy gave a quick glance to the playground where Jenny was now climbing a cargo net. "Keep it down a little about Jenny. I don't want her to know that we're talking about her." She now brought her voice down to a very low whisper. I really had to work hard to hear her.

"I had a dream that Flannery came to the school to visit me. He pulled me out of class like he used to, only now there weren't any other kids around. He grabbed me by the wrist and said that if I didn't do what he said, he was going to take my sister away from me forever."

She was fighting back the tears now. "That's not all," she continued, "look at this." She pulled her sleeve up and showed us her wrist. It had a very fresh looking bruise. It was in the shape of a hand, a very large hand. "He grabbed me just before I woke up. I thought it was just a dream, but it's a whole lot more."

Antoine and I looked at each other. It was a while before he finally said, "What do you want to do?"

"I want to fight, with you guys. I want to take him out. Messing with me is one thing, but now that he's threatened my sister...well, that's quite another."

"So you're in," I said. "Okay, we've got to come up with a plan."

She looked at me now, right in the eyes with the most intense stare I'd ever seen. "Do you have the hex bolt?"

"Yes," I replied.

"Where is it?"

"It's in the pocket of the shorts I was wearing during the last night of the tunnel cleanup."

"What's it doing in there?" Antoine asked.

"I put it in there because I thought that if I touched it with my bare skin I was going to be transported again. So I figured it would be best to keep it in my clothes for safekeeping, until the time came to use it again."

"Well," Suzy said, "You've gotta go get it. We have to go there – tonight."

"Tonight?" I asked. "No way, we can wait until tomorrow - "

"No, we can't," she said. "I have to go tonight. If I don't, I'm not so sure Jenny will be here tomorrow."

DISAPPEARANCE AT DARK

We would meet at the playground, under the maple tree. It would be after dinner, when the sun was just starting to dip below the horizon. It had to be dark when we latched onto the hex bolt, so that no one would see us disappear, or reappear.

Antoine and I arrived at about the same time. It was just after seven O'clock and the sun hadn't quite set. We waited for what seemed like forever for Suzy to show up. It wasn't like her to be late. Antoine even went so far as to check the tube slide to make sure she wasn't hiding.

We had just about given up on her when we heard a wild scream come from the other side of the school. We looked toward the far end of the building in the direction of the scream. Suzy was running around the corner and as soon as I could see her, I understood what she was saying. "They've got her!" she was yelling, "They've got Jenny. They took her!"

I reached into my pocket to get the hex bolt. I wanted to be prepared so we could go as soon as Suzy reached us. It wasn't there. I panicked and then remembered that I had slid it into my other pocket. I reached in and fumbled for a second. I was trying to be careful not to grab right on or I would be brought to the Fleshbots by myself.

As the hex bolt reached the top of my pocket my hand slipped. The hex bolt fell to the grass. Antoine was thinking the same thing I was thinking and we both reached over to pick it up. We were gone. Falling to who knows where...without Suzy.

*****

We hit the ground with a thud. It hurt like heck. I looked over to Antoine. He had been knocked unconscious. The hex bolt lay on the ground between the two of us. Before I had a chance to stand up I heard a familiar voice. "Get the skinny one and tie him to the door!" It was Flannery. He was right behind me.

In an instance Tingledowner and Giga grabbed Antoine by the wrists and ankles and hauled him over to the green, bolted door. Giga had some rope slung over her shoulder and she tied Antoine's feet and legs. They both lifted him up and took turns running the rope through chain shackles. He was dangling on the door, limp and lifeless.

While they were tying Antoine I looked to the middle of the floor and saw a young girl, tied at the feet and hands. It was Jenny!

"Stand up, fat boy!" Flannery said.

I stood.

Tingledowner and Giga now turned their attention to me. They let go of the ropes they were tying and Antoine slid about two feet before being jerked quickly and coming to rest. This shook him awake.

It took him a moment, but he soon realized what was going on .

"RUN!" he yelled.

"Yes, Coby, RUN!" Tingledowner said, mocking Antoine's plea. "Run as fast as you can, fatty. We'll catch you anyway. We know where you live remember?"

"You better do something, boy, or your family's going to wonder what happened to you?" Flannery said as he walked in my direction.

I looked around again. It was hot down here, and dark. The only ways out was the door Antoine was chained to or the hex bolt.

I was surrounded. Tingledowner was coming from my left, Flannery was coming from behind me, and Giga was coming from my right. I had to make a decision quickly.

"Coby," Antoine yelled. "Go get Suzy!"

Antoine was right. I had to get Suzy, but could I really leave him down here? Could I just leave Jenny there, tied up on the floor. How would I live with myself?

Tingledowner got to me first. I felt her finger on my wrist and I moved quickly away from her before she could close her grasp. I made my move.

I started to run toward the hex bolt. Antoine would be fine. I had to believe he would be. I also had to believe that Jenny would be alright until I could get Suzy and return.

There was no turning back now. They were right behind me and I could feel them closing in.

I was almost there. I could see the hex bolt in the distance.

"Get him!" Giga yelled from behind Tingledowner and Flannery. "He's getting away!"

She was right. I was getting away. I was so close now, just a few more steps. I reached out and grabbed the hex bolt.

I had it in my hand.

OPERATION GET SUZY AND SAVE THE DAY

I landed in the tunnels. I could see that most of the construction was underway. Some of the cement had already been poured and the passages directly below the school had been mostly filled.

Thankfully the passages away from the school remained open. I headed in the direction of the playground. When I got to the ladder that I thought was close to the maple tree, I climbed. I came up to a sewer grate that was located under a bench. I pushed on it, but couldn't get it open.

The maple tree was just on the other side of the playground. I could see it. I was almost there. Then I heard a whimper. I looked up and saw Suzy lying down on the bench. She was curled up in a ball and crying.

"Pssst," I said, "hey, down here."

She stopped crying and looked down at me. "What're you doing down there, Coby?"

"I came back to get you. But we don't have long. They've got your sister and Antoine. We need to hurry!"

I got the hex bolt from my pocket and reached through the grate toward Suzy. She reached down to grab it. Before she did I warned her, "As soon as you touch this you're going to be out of control for a little bit. It'll feel like you're falling. Tuck your head, so you don't get knocked out when you hit the ground." She nodded in the dark and then grabbed hold.

*****

I hit with a thud and it must've been really hard because I had to wait a second for the dust to settle. I looked over at Suzy and she was already on her feet.

"What was so hard about that?" she asked.

I hated not being athletic. "Nothing, I guess."

"Finally," the booming voice of Flannery came from behind us. "We were starting to think you weren't going to come back for your friends."

We turned around to face him. I'd almost forgotten how tall he was, how he towered over me.

"We're here!" said Suzy. "It's time to put an end to this."

"Oh, it'll never end," said Tingledowner, striding over to take her spot next to Flannery. "We'll just keep on coming back, no matter what you do."

"How's that possible?" I asked. "Antoine and I destroyed you last year."

Tingledowner looked at Flannery, "He really is stupid isn't he?"

"Not to mention, fat and slow," Flannery quipped and they both shared a metallic chuckle.

"Do you want to explain," Tingledowner asked, "or shall I?"

"Why don't we let Mrs. Giga take this one," Flannery said as he motioned for Giga to come join the conversation. "She has such a way with words. If anyone can get this imbecile to understand, it will be her."

Giga walked slowly over to the other two and took her place next to Flannery. Tingledowner appeared slightly miffed by the whole thing, but didn't say a word.

"Coby and Suzy," Giga started, "how have you been? I can imagine you've been feeling very frightened lately. Am I right?"

Neither Suzy, nor I responded. She continued, "Well, you should be. For as Mrs. Tingledowner just said a moment ago, you will never destroy us. You may slow us down for a little while, but you must not fool yourselves dearies...we will always come back."

"How?" I asked. I wanted her to get to the point. This cryptic message, solve the riddle type stuff was really starting to tick me off.

"You know what's on the other side of that door, don't you Coby?" Giga asked, and then without giving me time to finish, she continued. "This is our recovery chamber. You see, we're robots. We don't have human organs, we have parts. So, we'll never be killed – only broken. And you can always fix broken."

I felt a shudder go through my body. I looked over toward Antoine. He was still hanging from the door, but unconscious once again. I looked back to see Jenny. She was gone!

"Where's Jenny!" I demanded.

"Excuse me," Giga said, "but I am trying to explain something to you. Now, last year - "

"Tell me where she is!"

"I'll show you where she is if you don't shut your fat little mouth," she said. "We'll tie you up just like we did her."

Suzy was frantic and jittery, but quiet. She was still trying to play their game. She still thought that somehow if she just did what they wanted then she would be able to win. Not me. I was done playing this game.

"Yeah, yeah, yeah," I said. "We get it. We splashed you with water, you were broken, but not dead. I'm guessing someone came and got you after we returned to our normal lives and brought you down here. That's how you ended up in those chambers behind that green door. My guess is Jenny's back there too. And you sat in those chambers until you were strong enough to return to power and destroy Marley. Am I right?"

The three Fleshbots stood there motionless.

"So," I continued, "I'm going to go find Jenny and you three are going to do me a favor, okay? You're going to stand right there and keep your mouths shut while I do this."

"You really are a fool," Tingledowner said.

"I agree, Devindra," Flannery said. "I would have thought after last year he'd have learned a great deal about the choice to speak or keep quiet. Clearly he is as stupid as you said he was."

"There's only one thing left to do," Giga said. "Get 'em!"

*****

I looked at Suzy. "Run!" I said.

We both started running around. She went one way and I went the other. At first she had Flannery and Giga chasing after her and I had Tingledowner after me. Then at one point it changed and Giga and Tingledowner were chasing Suzy and Flannery was after me. I was starting to run out of breath...what else is new.

I yelled out the only two words I could muster in hopes that Suzy would understand them. "Green door!"

I started running toward the green door and thankfully so did she. "What are we going to do?" she asked.

"Open the door, get through it, and close it before they can get to us," I said.

"What about Antoine?" she asked.

"We have to get to Jenny first, then we can worry about Antoine."

She got to the door first and opened it. I ran through and she followed. It was strange. Flannery, Giga, and Tingledowner stopped chasing us.

We closed the door before they could follow us into the chamber room. We were home free.

Or, at least we thought we were.

*****

When we turned around we were greeted by what looked like twenty Fleshbots. All of whom were dressed differently. Some were dressed like janitors, some like business men, others like teachers. They were all different. And yet they all wanted to get us.

Out of the corner of my eyes I spotted Jenny. She was curled up in a little ball. It was just like Suzy the day Antoine and I had first met her behind the maple tree. Jenny was shaking and crying. Suzy and I ran to her.

"Are you alright?" Suzy asked her.

"I want to go home!" Jenny said.

Suzy looked back up at me. "What are we going to do about Antoine?"

I looked at the Fleshbots. They were getting closer.

"Listen," I said, "I have the hex bolt. I'm going to take it out of my pocket. As soon as I do, both of you need to grab it at the same time, got it?"

They both nodded.

I took the hex bolt from my pocket, took one last look at the approaching Fleshbots, and held it out for Suzy and Jenny.

We were off in a flash and back to the tunnels of Marley.

"Are we safe?" Jenny asked.

"I think so," said Suzy. "But what about Antoine?"

ONE LAST MISSION

"Alright," I said. "Here's the plan. I'm going to go back. You two are going to stay here and wait for me. Do not go home."

"Okay," said Suzy, "but what if you don't come back?"

"Wait for me until morning," I said. "If I don't show up by the time school starts let Mr. Shelman know what happened."

I took hold of the hex bolt and was off to rescue Antoine.

*****

It must've been my lucky trip, because on the fourth try, I finally got it right. I landed square on my feet and it felt incredible – until Tingledowner started running after me.

I ran away from her, the whole time trying to see if Antoine was still hanging from the green door. I couldn't get a good look. She kept chasing me away. After a few minutes Flannery came through the green door with Giga.

"Devindra," Flannery said, "you shouldn't try so hard to catch that little chunka munk."

Tingledowner stopped and put her hands on her hips. She looked at Flannery and then back toward me. "I suppose your right. We've got the smart one now anyways." She started walking back toward the green door that Flannery and Giga were in front of. Antoine was no longer there. The ropes and chains that held him in place were dangling freely, but he was gone. I knew instantly where he was.

"So what do you do now, boy?" Flannery asked.

"I don't know," I said.

"I honestly didn't think you'd be back," he said. "I didn't think you had it in you. You look like the kind of child who'd rather save his own hide."

"Well, I'm not!" I said. "What have you done with him?"

"Oh," Tingledowner interjected, "you know, a little of this and a little of that."

"Is he one of you now?" I asked.

"No," said Giga moving closer. "Not yet. We have to test him first."

"Can I see him?"

"Why on earth would we let you do that, boy?" Flannery asked, then turning to Tingledowner, "Devindra, would you be a sweetheart and go light the fire?"

"Absolutely," she said, a crazy smile formed on her face. "How hot do you want it?"

"Blazing," Flannery answered. "Now, Coby, this room is going to get very hot. Very, very hot. And I don't want you to get burned." He stopped talking for a moment and had a very good laugh. "Alright, maybe I do. Anyhow, just tell me one thing."

"What?" I asked.

"How is it that you came into possession of my hex bolt?"

"You're hex bolt?" I asked. It was starting to get really hot. A fire was burning all around us. Everywhere except in front of the green door.

"Yes," he said. "It belongs in my knee and I could've used it, what with all this running we've been up to tonight."

"Do you want it back?" I said.

"Certainly."

"What are you willing to give me for it?" I asked.

"I'll let you see your friend," he said. "How does that grab you?"

"Alright," I said. "That sounds good. It's just..."

"What?" Flannery asked, sounding irritated.

"Well, I can't touch it with my bare hand without heading back to Marley," I said. "It really is quite a dilemma."

"Well, Mr. Collins," Flannery started, I could see Giga and Tingledowner approaching me, one on each side. "What do you suggest we do?"

"You'll have to come and get it from my pocket yourself," I said. "You, Mr. Flannery, not them. Call off your dogs and come get it yourself."

"You snot nosed little pig!" Tingledowner said as she lunged at me.

"Devindra!" Flannery said and he began to run at Tingledowner.

Giga saw what Flannery was doing and also ran toward Tingledowner.

I started to run. I took a direct line between Flannery and Giga just as they approached Tingledowner. The three of them collided and fell to the ground.

"Get up!" Flannery yelled. "You fools, get up!"

I had a pretty good jump on them, there was no way they were going to catch me. I only had a few more feet to go.

I opened the green door and shut it quickly. I scanned the room for Antoine. It wasn't hard to find him. He looked very out of place among all of the Fleshbots. He was sitting on the floor and they were all huddled around him.

He looked up with horror on his face at all of the Fleshbots. He looked at me and yelled, "Coby!"

This was my chance. The Fleshbots all turned to face me and left a slight gap between themselves. It was going to be a tight squeeze, but maybe I could make it.

I took off running toward Antoine. I'd never played baseball before, but I'd seen baseball players slide into home plate. How hard could it be?

I slid face first into the dirt and got stuck in between two Fleshbots that looked like they might have been policemen at one point. They reached down and grabbed me.

"Antoine," I said, "reach out your hand and grab the bolt!"

I fumbled in my pocket for the bolt. The two Fleshbots began to pick me up and started to take me away from Antoine. The remaining Fleshbots started to close their circle so that Antoine couldn't escape.

I had my hand on the bolt and began to bring it forward out of my pocket. It hit the right arm of one of the policeman Fleshbots, and flew into the air. I watched it go up, up, up. I was about to attempt my second baseball move of all time and I was hoping it would go better than the first.

The hex bolt hung in the air forever. I'd heard people say 'keep your eye on the ball' when you're trying to catch something. It wasn't my eyes I was worried about, it was my hands.

It was starting to come down now. I felt like slow motion. It was turning over once...twice...three times. I reached out my hand, hoping like heck that it would just land where it needed to.

Finally it hit my hand. Something else hit my hand too. It felt like a finger, or maybe several fingers. I definitely had the bolt and I was heading back to the tunnels, but what else was with me?

OPEN YOUR EYES

I touched down with a thud. I hadn't quite perfected that. My eyes were closed. I was afraid to open them. Had I brought back one of the Fleshbot policemen, or worse, another Fleshbot teacher?

I could hear loud noises. It was the sound of engines and something scraping against cement. Then I heard a loud steady beep-beep-beep of a reverse signal.

"Hey kid," a man yelled, "open up your eyes and get out of the way. And get your friend outta here too. This is a construction site. You two can't be down here!"

I opened my eyes and saw Antoine getting to his feet.

"It was you!" I shouted. "Oh, Antoine, I'm so glad it was you. How are you? Are you okay?" I opened my arms to give him a hug.

"I'm fine," he said pushing me away.

"Get outta here!" the construction man yelled.

Antoine pointed up the ladder. "After you," he said.

"Almost," I said, "just one more thing." I looked at the hex bolt lying there on the cement floor between the two of us. I turned toward the cement mixer and positioned myself behind the bolt. I gave it a great kick and it landed in a pool of wet cement. It was just out of the reach of the man who was smoothing the cement with a trowel. I watched it slowly sink under.

"You blasted kids!" he yelled. "I'm gonna tell Principal Shelman, just you wait!"

"That's okay," I said, "I think I can handle him."

*****

Antoine and I climbed up the rope ladder and headed for the door. We walked out to the playground to see if Suzy and Jenny were there.

We found Suzy behind the maple, curled up in a ball and shaking. Jenny was not with her.

"Where's Jenny?" I asked her.

She didn't answer. She just kept rocking back and forth running her hands through her hair. Her shirt was all wet like she'd been crying for hours.

"Did she go home?" Antoine asked.

"Suzy," I said, firmly, "what's wrong?"

"He's got her," she said. "He's got her."

"Who's got her?" I asked.

"He's got her," was all she said. "He's got her."

COBY COLLINS
AND THE
DIARY OF
TINGLEDOWNER

MARLEY ELEMENTARY
ADVENTURES
VOLUME THREE

JUSTIN
JOHNSON

Contents

PROLOGUE

Dear Diary,

The draft coming through the floorboards is dreadful today. Papa said he'd come out with some more blankets for me, yet he did not.

I'd walk over to the house myself but it is raining buckets and I fear that I would catch pneumonia. I supposed I'll just sit here in the cold and wait for the storm to pass.

Dear Diary,

Papa did not come home last night. It was the strangest thing. Charlotte was so worried and afraid, she came from the main house to stay with me. She wanted to sleep in my bed, but I told her no. I told her to sleep on the floor, like a dog. Just like they would have me do.

She cried herself to sleep. I slept better than I'd ever slept before, knowing that Charlotte was miserable and papa was gone. Serves him right for trying, yet again, to take away any glimpse of happiness that I may have.

Dear Diary,

Charlotte emerged from the main house today with bruises on her arms and her hair chopped. I don't know why on earth papa would've cut her hair in that way.

Later in the day, papa came to visit me. I will spare you the details and only tell you that Charlotte and I are virtually indistinguishable from one another.

I tried to ask papa what had happened to him, but he wouldn't tell me. He only replied, "Everyone should have the power to live forever!"

I don't know what he meant, but I do know that it had a hold on him. Whatever that man in town had gotten him into had it's hold right on him — and I am scared.

WHAT DO WE DO NOW

Antoine and I climbed up the rope ladder and headed for the door. We walked out to the playground to see if Suzy and Jenny were there.

We found Suzy behind the maple, curled up in a ball and shaking. Jenny was not with her.

"Where's Jenny?" I asked her.

She didn't answer. She just kept rocking back and forth running her hands through her hair. Her shirt was all wet like she'd been crying for hours.

"Did she go home?" Antoine asked.

"Suzy," I said, firmly, "what's wrong?"

"He's got her," she said. "He's got her."

"Who's got her?" I asked.

"He's got her," was all she said. "He's got her."

*****

I was finally able to get her to snap out of it.

"Who has her!" I yelled.

Suzy stopped crying and looked deeply into my eyes. "Shelman," she said. "He's one of them!"

Antoine shot me a glance.

"What do you mean he's one of them?" I asked.

"He's a Fleshbot," Suzy said. "You told me to go to him if you didn't return before school started. I did," she wiped the tears from her eyes with her

155

sleeve. "He asked me what was wrong. I told him that you were in trouble and he pushed me out of his office, but not before he'd grabbed Jenny. He slammed the door in my face and when I finally got it open they were..."

"Gone," I helped her finish.

"Yeah," she said.

"Well, what do we do now?" Antoine asked.

"I don't know," I said.

"What do you mean you don't know!" Suzy snapped, "We go get her!"

"Right," I said, "I know that. I just don't know how."

"Take the hex bolt out of your pocket," Suzy said. "We'll go back and find Jenny."

I swallowed hard and looked at my feet. "There's just one problem with that."

"What?" she asked.

Antoine and I looked at each other.

"I don't have the hex bolt," I said.

"Where is it?"

"I thought we were done," I said. "I wanted to make sure they never returned. So I kicked the hex bolt into wet cement and it sank right in."

"Why did you do that?" Suzy growled, she looked like she was ready to punch me.

"It's okay, Suzy," Antoine said coming to my rescue. "Coby was just trying to do the right thing. He didn't know about Jenny. We'll have to think of something else."

"What do you suggest?" Suzy asked.

"Let's go back to Shelman's office," Antoine suggested. "Maybe we can find something there that will help us find Jenny."

"Alright," she said, "Let's go."

*****

School had ended for the day. Everyone was gone and the doors were locked. With the new security precautions the school had put in place, there was no way we were getting in through the door.

"Now what do we do?" Suzy whined.

Antoine looked around. He pointed down the side of the building. "Look," he said, "there."

A window had been left open. And right below it there was a ladder. It must've been our lucky day.

We rushed over to the ladder and began climbing. Antoine first, followed by Suzy, then me. It took me a second to get the hang of it and I almost fell. When I got to the top Suzy grabbed one arm and Antoine the other. Together they hoisted me through. I fell to the floor.

When I stood up I realized we were in Shelman's office. The door was locked and the room was empty. Suzy started snooping around. She looked under Shelman's desk and in his closet.

"What are you looking for?" I asked.

"Anything that will help us find Jenny."

"Over here," Antoine said. "What is it?" Suzy asked.

"A note," Antoine said. "From Shelman."

Antoine began to read the note.

I see by now you've found my ladder. How very clever of you to come looking for me. You should have kept the hex bolt, Coby.

I felt my face go flush. I should have kept it. He was right, and now Suzy might never see Jenny again. It was all my fault. Antoine continued reading.

Either way, that's neither here, nor there. You see, what's important is that I have Suzy's sister. And if you ever want to see her again you're going to have to work very, very hard. I've left you a little something in the top right hand drawer of my desk. Find it and be on your way.

-S

"Be on your way where?" Antoine asked. He scratched his head, trying to put it all together.

"It doesn't matter where," Suzy said, "we have to find my sister." She grabbed the handle of the desk drawer and opened it so fast that a stack of index cards and a blue marker flew out onto the floor.

"What do you think we're looking for?" I asked. "He left us a little something," I said repeating the line from the note.

Whatever it was, it would be difficult to find. This drawer was full of stuff. It had staplers, staples, paper clips, pencils, sticky notes, and even some toys. We took everything out and threw it on the floor. And then Suzy got it.

She reached out and grabbed something. It was hard to tell what it was, but in the blink of an eye she was gone.

"Where'd she go?" I asked.

"I don't know," Antoine said. "But it looks like she found what Shelman wanted her to. I just hope she comes back and - "

In an instant Suzy was back.

"Where'd you go?" Antoine asked her.

She was holding onto a key. A very small key that looked like it went to a very small lock.

"Grab on," she said. "You've gotta see this."

WHERE AND WHEN

When we arrived at our destination, Antoine and Suzy were on their feet and ready to go. I had to pick myself up and dust off.

We took a second to look around. We were in an old room. The floorboards were creaky and the walls were made of logs. It was dark and cold and smelled damp. There was a lit candle in a brass holder on the table next to a very small bed.

"What do you think this place is?" I asked.

"It's hard to say," Antoine said.

"It's a house," Suzy replied. "A very old house."

"Thanks for that insight," Antoine shot back.

"Anytime," said Suzy.

Walking around the room felt strange. This was different from the hex bolt. That took us to a different place, but this key seemed to take us to a different time entirely.

"Do you think anyone's here?" Suzy asked.

"I don't really want to find out," I said.

"Neither do I," Antoine agreed.

Suzy walked over to the door in the corner of the room and put her hand on the knob.

"Wait!" Antoine yelled in a forced whisper.

"What?" she said.

"What if someone's here?"

"Well, then we'll have a better chance out there than in here," she said. "Look around. There are no windows in this room."

She was right. It hadn't dawned on us before but this room seemed dark for a reason.

"That makes no sense," Antoine said. "You have the key. We don't have to go out there."

"I'm not going back without Jenny," Suzy said.

"You'd better give me the key then," Antoine said. "Because if someone or something starts giving chase, you can bet your butt I'm going back."

"Alright," Suzy said. She handed the key to Antoine and he put it in his pocket. I walked over to where Antoine was standing. I liked Suzy and all, but if something happened I wanted to be closest to whoever had the key.

"Happy?" she asked.

"Not really," Antoine said.

Suzy walked back to the door in the corner. She opened it and we were instantly blinded by sunlight.

*****

It was quiet. The only sounds were those of the birds chirping and a gentle breeze blowing through the trees.

"What do you see?" Antoine asked Suzy.

"I can't yet," she said, squinting her eyes.

Antoine and I started to move toward the door to get a better look.

162

It was a field full of dandelions and grass as high as I'd ever seen. There were no places in Marley with grass this high, at least none I was aware of. On the other side of the field, a few hundred feet away, was another house.

"Do you think we should go out?" I asked.

"Let's go," Suzy said.

The house we were in was missing its front steps. She jumped down into the grass below. Antoine jumped down next. Then I jumped down and ended up with grass stains on my shorts and knees.

We started walking toward the other house. I took a look back.

"That's odd," I said. Suzy and Antoine were well ahead of me and didn't hear. "Hey guys!" I yelled. They turned around. "Doesn't this look a little strange to you? It's not even a house. It's just a room. A square room, built out of logs, in the middle of a field, a few hundred feet from a real house."

"That is weird," Antoine said, "I wonder who sleeps in there?"

"Let's go over to the big house and see if we can get some answers," Suzy said.

High grass stinks. It wasn't a long walk, but the grass was fighting me every step of the way. The sun was beating down on me and by the time we arrived at the big house I was covered in sweat.

"I need a drink of water," I panted as we arrived at steps of the front porch.

Suzy walked up the steps and knocked on the door. There was no answer. She knocked again. No answer.

"I think it's safe to go in," she said, pushing the door open.

"Suzy wait - " Antoine started, but it was too late. Suzy had already gone in.

"Do you think we should go help her?" I asked.

"Probably," Antoine said.

We climbed the steps and entered the front door of the cabin. We were in one big open space. The floor, as with the room in middle of the field, were made of creaky wooden boards.

"I am so thirsty," I said, and started looking for a sink.

"I think you're out of luck," Antoine said, pointing around the kitchen. There was no sink, just a metal tub in the corner of the room. There was no faucet or outlets.

"Forget *where* we are? I'm wondering *when* we are?" I said.

"I don't know," Antoine said, "but let's try to find out where Suzy's gone off to."

We walked through a doorway that separated the main room of the house to a smaller room with two beds and a small wood-burning stove.

Suzy was staring at a nightstand that had a candle burning in a holder. She was still.

"What is it?" Antoine asked.

"We have to leave," she said.

"Why?" I asked.

"We have to leave right now."

Antoine and I walked over to the nightstand and saw a book in the faint candlelight. On the cover of the book were the words:

Property of Jacob Flannery.

BACK TO THE SOLITARY ROOM

"Who's Jacob Flannery?" I asked.

Suzy and Antoine both shot back looks of disbelief.

"Are you serious?" Suzy said. "You've never seen that name before? Think long and hard, Coby."

I was thinking. I only knew one Flannery and he was a –

"Oh my," I said. "We have to get out of here!"

"Wait a minute," Antoine said. "Maybe this is just a Flannery, not the Flannery."

"Right, Antoine," said Suzy, "It's just a happy coincidence that we grab onto this key that Shelman – a Fleshbot – left for us and we end up here in the middle of, I don't know where. And then we find ourselves in a house that has a book labeled 'property of Jacob Flannery'. And, as it just so happens, the only Flannery any of us know is also a Fleshbot." She paused a second, "Yeah, you're probably right, it could just be a Flannery."

"You don't have to be sarcastic about it," Antoine replied.

"Well don't be so stupid."

"Hey guys," I said, stepping in before things got any worse, "why don't we just cool it a bit. We have a lot of questions here that need to be answered and fighting isn't going to get us any closer to finding Jenny."

Suzy and Antoine stopped and looked at each other.

"Sorry," Suzy said.

"It's okay," said Antoine.

"Let's take a look at the other bed," I said.

We walked over to the other bed and noticed that it was much smaller than Flannery's. There was a nightstand and a candle, which was not lit. Other than that, there was nothing.

"This looks like a kid's bed," said Antoine. "Do you remember the bed in the other room?"

"Yeah," said Suzy, "it was small like this one. You know, I think I remember seeing a book on the nightstand next to that bed."

"You think we should go back?" I said.

"That's what I'm thinking," Suzy said.

*****

We walked across the field again and climbed into the room.

Suzy went right to the nightstand.

"I knew it!" she said. She held up a small, black book.

"What's that dangling off the edge?" Antoine asked.

"It's a lock," said Suzy, rolling her eyes. "Honestly, haven't you boys ever seen a diary before?"

168

"Oh, yeah," Antoine said, "It's just with the sun coming in the...and the room being so..."

"Right," Suzy said.

"If it's locked, how are we supposed to get it open?" I asked.

"I don't know," Suzy said. "There's got to be a key here somewhere. Look around. We need a really tiny key."

Antoine started looking under the bed. I looked near a tiny little dresser. Suzy started to open the drawers of the nightstand. Nothing.

"Wait a second," Antoine said. "Didn't we come here with a key?"

Suzy shut the drawer to the nightstand and stood up straight. "You're right." She reached into her pocket. "It's gone!"

"No it's not," said Antoine. "You gave it to me, remember?"

He reached into his pocket and pulled out the key and disappeared instantly.

"He'll be back," I said noticing that Suzy looked a little shocked. "You did the same thing when you found the key in Shelman's office."

"Right," She said.

Suzy and I waited in silence for several minutes.

But Antoine did not come right back.

We were growing worried, but there was nothing we could do but wait. We didn't have a key to get us back. All we had was each other in this small room.

"Does it say anything on the cover of the book?" I asked, trying to keep my mind off Antoine.

"No, not that I can see."

"How about the back?"

"Nope, nothing," she said.

The minutes kept creeping by and we waited and waited and waited for Antoine to return. I continued to sweat and Suzy's eyes began fill with tears.

"It'll be okay," I said.

"No it won't," Suzy said. "How am I ever going to get Jenny back? What will I tell my parents?" She stared past me out into the open field of grass and dandelions. "Will I ever see my parents again?"

Just as suddenly as this thought came across her lips, Antoine reappeared.

"Where have you been?" Suzy asked forcefully.

"Yeah," I said, "You had us worried sick."

"We have to go back," Antoine said.

"What? No way, I'm staying here until we find Jenny," said Suzy stubbornly.

"No," Antoine said, "You don't understand. You won't find her here."

"What are you talking about? Why are we here then?"

"I don't know," Antoine answered, "but I think we have to look at who helped us get here. It was Shelman that left us the note and the key, right?"
Suzy and I nodded.

"Why would he send us to the exact location of the person we were trying to rescue. He said in his note that we would have to work 'very, very hard.' Well, we haven't worked very hard at all, have we?"

"What's your point?" Suzy was getting impatient. I understood why, but Antoine was on to something. "My point is," he said very slowly, "that we were sent here for a reason. There is something we were meant to find – and it was never going to be Jenny. It had to be something else, something smaller. And, perhaps, the key that transported us here was a clue."

"You mean the diary," I said. "We were meant to find the diary and bring it back."

"Bingo was his name-o," grinned Antoine. I hated it when he did that.

"So what's that going to do for us?" Suzy asked, still unwilling to accept Antoine's theory.

"I don't know yet," said Antoine. "But I do know that we need to get that book quickly and head back to Shelman's office right away."

"You still haven't told us why we have to do that," Suzy said.

"Because," Antoine said, "when I went back, I was directly under Shelman's desk. And he was there, sitting down, talking on the phone. I stayed and listened to what he was saying. He was setting up a secret meeting, for tonight, in the Gym. From what I could gather, it sounded like it was going to be a meeting to decide the fate of Jenny. He kept saying 'the Trudell girl.'"

"Then it's settled," said Suzy, wiping the tears from her eyes and standing up taller than I'd ever seen her stand. She had a look of determination on her face, like nothing, not even Shelman, was going to be able stop her. "Put the key on the bed."

Antoine shook the key from his pocket, being very careful not to touch it, and it fell onto the edge of the bed.

Suzy reached past me and grabbed the book. We gathered around the key and looked into each other's eyes.

"Here goes nothin'," she said.

CRAMPED DESK
SMELLY FEET

I had no idea where we were going to land and I was preparing myself for the worst. However, nothing could have prepared me for this.

We landed hard under Shelman's desk. All three of us, cramped in there, where his feet went when he was sitting at it.

"Zenu, zenu, zenu...how many times have I told you not to get involved in the trivial stuff. Just let it go my man – and make sure you're over here in time for our little meeting," Shelman was still in here! Suddenly, I heard the phone touch down on the receiver and the metal of the desk popped noisily as Shelman spun himself around and put his feet down on the floor. He turned and sat in his chair and sent his feet in our direction.

I know the situation was pretty serious, but I had to stop thinking about it for just a moment when I caught my first whiff of Shelman's feet. Oh boy, did they stink. I tried to hold my breath and get my mind back on track.

I looked in Antoine's direction. He had his face buried in the crook of his arm. I turned toward Suzy.

She seemed un-phased by the smell. She just stared at Shelman's legs, anger in her eyes.

Shelman picked up the phone again and began dialing. It was several seconds before anybody answered.

"Lenny," I heard Shelman begin, "how are you?"

Lenny must've told him something important because I heard Shelman's pen scratching against some paper, like he was writing something down.

"That's great to hear," Shelman continued. "Alright, big man. Well, obviously we're disappointed that you can't make it, but we all understand and wish you the best."

He put the receiver down again and stood up. Finally, I could begin to breath again. I was starting to get dizzy and thought that I might pass out.

We remained perfectly still until we heard him take four steps toward the door and shut it behind him as he left.

"That was close," said Suzy.

"Agreed," Antoine replied.

"Holy cow, did you guys smell those feet?" I asked. "I mean, take a shower man!"

My comment was met with un-amused stares.

"Alright, take it easy," I said. "I was just saying what's on my mind."

"Well do us a favor next time, Coby," Suzy said, "and don't."

"Okay."

"Do you think it's safe?" Antoine asked.

"He's been gone a few minutes," Suzy said. "I think we're probably okay."

We piled out from beneath the desk and took a moment to stretch. I looked down at myself. I was covered in sweat and dirt and grass. Then I looked at Antoine and Suzy. They looked like they'd just finished watching Saturday morning cartoons – not a spot on them.

"What's the plan now?" Antoine asked looking at Suzy.

"We need to get into this diary and figure out what it means," said Suzy. "But, I don't know how to open it without being transported again."

Antoine started scratching his head. I looked in the direction of Shelman's desk.

"Hey guys," I said, "take a look at this. Did you hear Shelman writing something down when he was on the phone with Lenny?"

"Yeah," they said.

"Well, he must've known we were here."

"Why do you say that?" Antoine asked.

"Take a look for yourself," I said, handing Antoine a sheet of paper.

He read it out loud:

Hope you were cozy under there.
I see you found what you were looking for. Use a piece of fabric to hold onto the key.

-S

P.S. We're having a little get together in the gymnasium around five o'clock. It would be terrific if you could join us.

"She's here!" Suzy exclaimed. "I know she is! She's right here in the school! Let's go get her!"

"Hold on a minute," said Antoine. "Let's not rush into anything now."

"Easy for you to say," she said, "they don't have your sister."

"I understand that, but we can't just go rushing into the gym, without thinking things through. Besides," Antoine said, looking at the clock, "It's only three o'clock. We've got another two hours to wait."

"Well, what do you suggest we do?"

Antoine looked down at the note again and then reached for the diary in Suzy's hand. He then walked over to the desk and took a tissue from the box of Kleenex.

"Key please," he said to Suzy.

"I don't have it," she said.

"Key please," he said to me.

"It's in my pocket," I said.

"Well, this is awkward," he said. "Stay perfectly still Coby."

He took the tissue between his thumb and index finger and slowly reached into my pocket.

"Stop!" Suzy yelled.

"What?" Antoine said.

176

"Seriously, are boys always so stupid?" She took the tissue from Antoine's hand and gave it to me. "You reach into your own pocket and then hand the key over to Antoine."

"Oh, yeah," I said nodding my head in Antoine's direction, "that makes more sense."

"Honestly," Suzy rolled her eyes.

I grabbed the key with the tissue and handed it over to Antoine. He placed the key into the lock and began to turn it.

THE DIARY

The lock opened surprisingly easy given its age. I don't know how old the book must've been, but it was tattered and the edges were frayed. The lock had little deposits of rust here and there.

Antoine turned the cover back to reveal the first page.

Property of Suzy Flannery

"Who is Suzy Flannery?" I asked. It stood to reason that this was Flannery's daughter, but what did that mean? And why were we supposed to find this book?

"I don't know," said Antoine. "Does anyone else think it's odd that her name is spelled exactly the same as Suzy's?"

I looked at Suzy. She'd gone white as a ghost.

"What is it Suzy?" Antoine asked. "What's wrong?"

"I don't know," She said. She furled her eyebrows and rubbed her forehead with her index finger and thumb. "Do you think this...I mean, am I supposed to...am I related to Flannery somehow?"

"No," Antoine said. "I don't think so. Get that out of your head. Your last name's Trudell, not Flannery. The first name's just a coincidence."

This seemed to put Suzy at ease a little, but she was more determined now to press on.

"Turn the page, Antoine."

He did and we began reading Suzy Flannery's diary.

Dear Diary,

The draft coming through the floorboards is dreadful today. Papa said he'd come out with some more blankets for me, yet he did not.

I'd walk over to the house myself but it is raining buckets and I fear that I would catch pneumonia. I supposed I'll just sit here in the cold and wait for the storm to pass.

Suzy
September 3, 1767

"1767?" Antoine shouted. "Holy cow this thing is old."

"I haven't gotten that far yet," I said.

"So," said Suzy ignoring me, "do you think this means that we went back to 1767 this morning?"

"Oh," I said, "just got there. Wow, do you think we went back to 1767 this morning?"

"That's what Suzy just said," Antoine fired. "Try to keep up will ya!"

"Let's keep reading," said Suzy, sensing that my feelings had been hurt.

Antoine turned the page.

Dear Diary,

The storm has passed, the sun is out and I've just had the most wonderful day! A boy named Joseph Tingledowner came to visit me!

I met him last week when I was wandering through the woods looking for something to do.

Oh, he is just the nicest boy. He talks softly, about gentle things, not like papa. And he listens and hangs on every single word I speak. Oh, how I love him!

Suzy
October 14, 1767

"Tingledowner!" I said. "Are you kidding me? Do you think this could be Tingledowner's mom and dad?"

"Possibly," said Antoine. "I do think we're getting a little closer to finding out exactly why we were meant to find this book."

"Turn the page," said Suzy. She was chomping at the bit. She could feel us getting closer to something that would help us find Jenny.

Dear Diary,

Papa came by today. He told me to forget about Joseph Tingledowner and that I would never see him again. When I asked him why and what he meant, he simply laughed and said, "You'll see."
I watched through my door as he climbed upon his horse and headed for the village. I don't know what he intends to

do, but my mind feels uneasy. My heart breaks at the thought of never seeing Joseph again. If there is anyway this can be undone, let it be so.

Suzy
November 4, 1767

"Alright," said Antoine, "so there was something not so great about old Joey T, and her father was going to put a stop to it."

"Something doesn't feel right," said Suzy.

"What do you mean?" Antoine asked.

"Well," she said, "what I mean is, her father is going to town to make sure that she never sees Joey again. But that doesn't complete the connection here. We're supposed to learn something from this book. This just doesn't make any sense at all."

"We're not done yet," I said. "We should keep reading."

Dear Diary,

Papa did not come home last night. It was the strangest thing. Charlotte was so worried and afraid, she came from the main house to stay with me. She wanted to sleep in my bed, but I told her no. I told her to sleep on the floor, like a dog. Just like they would have had me do.

She cried herself to sleep. I slept better than I'd ever slept before, knowing that Charlotte was miserable and papa was gone. Serves him right for trying, yet again, to take away any glimpse of happiness that I may have.

Suzy
November 5, 1767

"Well, we can't stop there," said Antoine turning the page.

"Are you sure?" I said. "My eyes are starting to burn." All this reading with no sleep was really getting to me.

"Tough," said Suzy.

Dear Diary,

Papa finally came home today. It's been the most glorious three days of my life – except, of course, when I'm with Joey.

Something must've happened to him in town. He looked all haggard and he was different somehow.

He said he met a man and that man gave him the most incredible thing. When I asked what it was he told me not to be so stupid and he grabbed Charlotte and took her back to the main house.

I watched as they walked through the field. Charlotte was screaming that his grip was too tight, but he just kept dragging her through the tall grass and dandelions. He hoisted her up onto the porch and threw her through the door and then took one last look at me before slamming the door shut.

Were his eyes glowing red, or did I just imagine it?

Suzy
November 8, 1767

There was no discussion about this passage as Antoine turned to the next entry.

Dear Diary,

Charlotte emerged from the main house today with bruises on her arms and her hair chopped. I don't know why on earth papa would've cut her hair in that way.
Later in the day, papa came to visit me. I will spare you the details and only tell you that Charlotte and I are virtually indistinguishable from one another.
I tried to ask papa what had happened to him, but he wouldn't tell me. He only replied, "Everyone should have the power to live forever!"

I don't know what he meant, but I do know that it had a hold on him. Whatever that man in town had gotten him into had it's hold right on him — and I am scared.
Suzy,
November 9, 1767

Dear Diary,

Charlotte and papa are coming. I fear I don't have much time left, for I can see them walking across the field and they don't look like they are of this world. Where is their skin...they are all metal. Their eyes are glowing and they have the most terrible smiles wrapped around their faces. I fear it is too late for me. I fear the worst is yet to come. They are coming to do to me what has been done to them and I don't want to become one of them. I am not one of them. I will never be

The writing stopped there. The diary was over. A simple stray ink splotch coming from the final word was all that was left of Suzy Flannery.

We stood there motionless and silent for minutes, each one of us trying to sort this whole thing out.

Finally, Suzy spoke.

"One thing's for sure," she said, "Jacob Flannery is *the* Jacob Flannery. And he had two daughters and turned both of them into Fleshbots. But where are they?"

"I have a theory," Antoine said, breaking his silence.

"What's that?" I asked.

He looked up at the clock. "It's almost five O'clock now. My bet is Suzy and Charlotte are going to be in that Gymnasium."

"We better get going," Suzy said.

Antoine closed the diary and put it in his pocket, Suzy grabbed the key with the Kleenex and put it in her pocket. I took the lock, because, hey, why not? And then the three of us began our stealthy march toward the Gym.

TO THE GYM

The office was empty as we poked our heads through Shelman's door. We walked out and looked through the doors into an empty hallway.

"This is going to be easier than I thought," I said.

"Shhhh," Antoine and Suzy both scolded.

"Sorry," I said.

We kept walking in the direction of the gym. A door opened at the far end of the hallway and several important looking figures emerged.

"In there," Antoine said, shoving me into the bathroom. Suzy ducked in after us.

"How many of them did you see?" she asked.

"There must've been at least ten, maybe more," Antoine answered.

"What do we do now?" I asked.

"We sit wait - until we can be sure we won't be seen," said Antoine.

I could tell the minutes felt like days for Suzy. She became impatient.

"Can't we just go already?"

"Suzy," Antoine said, "I know you want to find your sister. We need to be careful. Otherwise, everything we've done to this point will be wasted and we'll end up members of the Fleshbot Legion."

I walked to the door and stuck my head into the hallway. It looked like the coast was clear. The clock on the wall read 4:59.

"I have to think that anyone who's going to be there would be there by now."

"I agree," said Suzy.

Antoine reluctantly walked toward the door and took a look. He motioned for us to follow him. We walked in the direction of the gym, slowly and quietly.

The far doors were left open and we could hear a great deal of commotion. The murmurs of side conversations and the clatter of people finding their seats could be heard.

We finished our journey to the gym with a short sprint toward the open doors. We didn't dare go in, rather we took our positions hiding behind the doors so we could hear what was going on.

I could see through a crack in the door that there were hundreds of Fleshbots piling onto the bleachers. In the center of the gym was a podium. Behind it, Shelman was talking to Flannery, looking over some papers. Flannery set the papers down, gave Shelman a hearty pat on the shoulder and handshake. He then returned to his seat, which was in a special row of chairs set out on the gym floor.

There were only four chairs. The two on the end were empty. No doubt one of those belonged to Shelman. Flannery was in one of the middle seats. He was sitting next to a very tall, gaunt looking man with long brown, straggly hair that was pulled back in a ponytail. Both men wore blue suits with red ties, which was different from the men and women in the crowd. They were just wearing normal, everyday clothes.

"Do you see Jenny?" Suzy whispered.

I looked around and tried to find her, but from this vantage point I was unable to.

"No," I said. "I can't see her from here."

She sighed a loud sigh and her shoulders dropped. Antoine started to console her when Shelman's voice boomed through the microphone.

THE FLESHBOT LEGION

"Welcome, friends," Shelman said as he began the meeting. "It is so nice to see so many of you could make it. I know Marley can be quite a trek for some of you...am I right, Willy?"

Shelman took a second to pause, wink, and point at a man in the crowd. "Yer darn tootin'" said the man named Willy. He was wearing overalls and had very few teeth. His red hair fell into his face as he laughed and pointed back at Shelman.

"We are here because of a girl. A very young girl that has just recently come into our possession. She is so young, in fact, that some of our Legion has declared her unfit for Conversion."

At this, a mixture of cheers and hissing erupted from the Fleshbots seated in the bleachers. Shelman let this go for a few minutes and then stifled it. "SILENCE!" his voice boomed. "Sit down and gather yourselves. We have much to discuss."

The crowd did as it was told, sitting down and looking forward at Shelman without uttering another word.

"I was just speaking with my esteemed colleague, Mr. Jacob Flannery, before we began today. He is of the notion that this girl would make a fine Fleshbot for us. He said he would recommend her very highly based on his experience with the sister."

Shelman looked toward Flannery, "Is that correct Jacob?" Flannery nodded his head. Some of the Fleshbots in the crowd shook their heads in disagreement, while others clapped their hands and nodded their approval.

"And Zenu," Shelman said, nodding to the man with the scraggly hair next to Flannery, "has also agreed that Ms. Jenny Trudell would make a lovely addition to the Fleshbot family. In fact, he thinks we may be able to get a few more as well."

At this point, a man in the crowd stood up. He was well dressed and clean cut. "Now just wait a minute," he shouted from his seat. "I'm looking around and I see quite a few of us who don't agree with this, most of us in fact. And yet –"

"Sit down, Fred," said Shelman calmly from behind the podium, "or you're going to wish you had."

"I will not sit down and take this! What you're doing is wrong. We have Legion Laws to live by that have been in place for thousands of years. And just because you think this five year old would make a great Fleshbot, you're willing to break them. I will not stand for it!" He then turned toward the crowd. "Stand up with me, please. I'm begging you. Stand up for what is right!"

Everyone in the gym stared at Fred. He had made his plea and was now looking for someone, anyone to stand with him. No one did.

"Are you finished, Fred?" Shelman asked.

Fred did not speak. He stood tall and did not sit down.

"Very well then," Shelman said, nodding in the direction of the far gymnasium door.

Two men dressed like policemen walked toward Fred. As they got closer the people around Fred all put their heads down. They looked at their feet, rather than see what was about to happen to him.

"Don't look away," Fred yelled, "that's what they want. They want you to bow down to them, like sheep. Stand up and tell them what they're doing is wrong."

The two men grabbed Fred and pulled him down from the bleachers and walked him toward the far doors. I couldn't see them after that. All I heard was a terrible scream and then the doors flew open and Fred was tossed into the hallway. His body lay lifeless on the floor.

The doors swung shut and the meeting continued as though nothing had happened.

"Zenu," Shelman motioned a beckoning hand, "why don't you come up and tell the nice people here what you're thinking."

Zenu rose. He was even taller than I'd imagined. He must have been a full foot taller than Shelman, at least.

He walked over to the podium, adjusted the microphone and spoke. His voice was very soft.

"Hello," he said to the gathered crowd. "Um, well, what I was thinking, really, was that we could, um, you know convert Jenny. And this would," he turned and coughed into the crook of his elbow, "um, also, possibly allow us to, um, get her sister – Suzy's her name, right Jacob?"

Flannery nodded. He folded his arms across his chest and a full smile formed beneath his beard.

"Yeah,um," Zenu continued, "we may also be able to get the Collins girl. Jill, right?"

Again Flannery nodded.

"I hear she's quite smart, and, um, since her brother is kind of, um, following us, it would probably be fairly easy to get her, too."

I looked at Suzy. She was gritting her teeth and clenching her fists. Antoine was already holding her back. She looked like she was ready to run right into their meeting and try to stop the whole thing.

"Get a grip," I whispered to her. "If you're not careful they're going to know we're here!"

She glared at me. "They already know we're here," she said. And then she broke free from Antoine's grip and ran right into the gym and up to the podium.

There was an audible gasp and Zenu turned to see what was happening. He looked down at Suzy and then turned back to the crowd. "Um, everybody, I'd, um, like you to meet, Suzy Trudell."

He then turned back to Suzy. "Thought you'd, um, make it easy on us eh?"

"Where's my sister?" Suzy demanded.

"Safe," Shelman said standing up and walking over to Suzy.

"I didn't ask if she was safe," Suzy cried, "I asked where she was!"

"Just calm down my dear, and maybe you'll find out."

Antoine looked at me and asked, "What do we do?"

"I think we have to go in after her," I said. "I don't really know, I wasn't counting on this."

"Fine," said Antoine. He walked slowly into the gym and stood behind Suzy. I followed hesitantly. The gasps and applause were deafening as the three of us now stood there, united against the most powerful men in all of the Fleshbot Legion.

One of the women from the crowd yelled, "Get 'em!"

Shelman held up his hand, signaling the crowd to remain seated. He wanted to talk. Flannery was coming up behind him.

"We can handle this in a dignified way," said Shelman, speaking into the microphone so everyone could hear. "Or, we can do it in a way that would result in a most embarrassing end for the three of you. Which do you choose?"

"Where's my sister?" Suzy asked, unwilling to change the subject.

"I will tell you that she is not in Marley. In fact, the next time she is in Marley, she will be one of us."

"You sent us away from here...you said in your note that we would find her," Suzy said, tears started to form in her eyes. "You lied to us."

Shelman faced the crowd. "This is simply not true. There was no lie told, quite the opposite. I stated that they would have to work very hard if they wanted to see her sister again. Clearly, interrupting our meeting in this way is not what one would call working very hard, is it Ms. Trudell?"

Antoine pulled the diary from his pocket and held it up high. "What's this?"

"You know what that is," said Flannery stepping forward. "Why would you ask such a stupid question?"

"I didn't mean, *what's this?*" Antoine stuttered, "I meant, why would we be sent to retrieve this if you were only going to convert Jenny anyway."

Upon seeing what was in Antoine's hand, the voice of a woman emerged from the crowd, "Where'd you get that! Tell me where you got that!"

I was shocked. The voice from the crowd was a voice I'd heard before...all too often as a matter of fact. And when she stood up I could clearly see that things were about to get messed up.

Devindra Tingledowner started down the bleachers. She'd been sitting near the top and seemed to make it to the bottom in record time. She was rushed, yet graceful and was standing between us and them within seconds.

"Where'd you get this?" She asked Antoine.

"We brought it back from a small cabin in the middle of a field," Suzy answered. "Why?"

"It's mine," Tingledowner said, "It belongs to me!"

"What are you talking about?" Antoine asked, "It says 'Property of Suzy Flannery' on the inside."

"Yes," Tingledowner said, turning to stare at Flannery, "I am Suzy Flannery!" she announced.

Jacob Flannery shook his head, "I don't know what she's talking about."

"Yes you do papa," Tingledowner said. "It's me Suzy, you're un-loved daughter. Isn't that right? Do you remember, papa, how you made me live in a room away from the house, while you and Charlotte lived peacefully. I was out there, all by myself...for years, with nothing. Until you went to the village and brought back this book for me. It became my friend, my most trusted companion. I told it everything."

"She's lying," Flannery said. "I know this woman only as Devindra Tingledowner, teacher and Fleshbot."

"You're a snake," Tingledowner fired back. "You came back from the village after three days and you'd changed. Do you remember? You took Charlotte and converted her, and then the next day you did the same to me. As time went on you told us that we could not be known as your daughters and had to establish our own identities to be part of the Legion. Do you remember that?"

Flannery now began sweating profusely. He reached for his handkerchief and wiped his forehead. "Wait a minute," Suzy interrupted. "Is that why you changed your name?"

"Yes," Tingledowner said. "He wanted us both to be called Giga, but if I was not going to be a Flannery anymore, there was no way I was going to share a name with Charlotte."

"And you chose Tingledowner because of Joseph?" Antoine asked.

"Precisely," Tingledowner said, "anything to upset my father. He had his favorite and I was clearly not it. I thought long and hard about the one thing that would upset him most." She stared right into Flannery's eyes as she said, "And taking the name of Joseph Tingledowner, the boy my papa forbade me to see, was the thing I thought would hurt him most."

"So, wait a minute," I said, "Giga's your sister?"

"At one time, yes. But not anymore!"

Shelman tried to intervene. "Devindra, why don't we just calm down. You can have your little book and take your seat."

"No," she said. "I'm finished with this! I will no longer call myself a Fleshbot! I am no longer Devindra Tingledowner – I am Suzy Tingledowner!"

With that she grabbed the diary from Antoine's hands and took flight. She ran out of the gym. Suzy, Antoine and I followed. Shelman, Flannery and Zenu also took chase, along with some of the Fleshbots from the bleachers.

We left the gym and turned right down a hallway. They were still on us, then we turned left. We were starting to lose them. Finally, we took another left and Tingledowner ducked into an empty classroom.

We followed and shut the door.

Crouched behind the door we could hear the mob rush past.

When we turned back to Tingledowner, she had a gentle presence about her. She was holding the diary like a young girl, full of excitement.

"I want to go back," she said.

THE RETURN

The three of us stood there, staring at her, in disbelief. This woman, who just last year had started my life on this nightmare, and who just yesterday was chasing me around, trying to kill me, was now so sweet and innocent.

"What do you mean you want to go back?" Suzy asked.

"Precisely that," Tingledowner said, "I know one of you must have the key. I wish to go back home."

"Why should we help you?" Antoine piped up. "You started all of this for us."

"That's right," Tingledowner said, "I did. And I can help you end it."

"How?" asked Suzy.

"Easy," said Tingledowner, "I can tell you where your sister is."

"Okay," Suzy said cooly, "where is she?"

"Not so fast," said Tingledowner, reaching her hand out for the key.

Suzy pulled the key, wrapped in Kleenex from her pocket and started to hand it over. Tingledowner's hand was just about to touch the key, when Suzy pulled it back.

"Tell me where Jenny is first."

"No."

"Why not?"

"Because," Tingledowner said, "if I tell you where she is, you may never give me the key."

"Okay, well what do you suggest we do?"

"You come back with me," said Tingledowner. "Once I'm back, I'll tell you about Jenny and you can have the key. I won't need it with Charlotte and papa here. There will be no way anyone can see my diary."

"That sounds reasonable," I said.

Suzy was not so sure. She looked at Tingledowner and then at the key.

"Come on Suzy," Antoine urged, "it's the only way."

"Alright," Suzy said, "but you'd better tell me where she is when we get there."

"I promise," Tingledowner said as a smile came over her face.

Suzy held out her hand, the tissue unwrapped and the key laying on top. All four of us gathered around and counted to three, touched it and were on our way.

*****

We all fell hard on the wooden floor of the cabin. Suzy, Antoine and I stood up and looked around for a sign of Tingeldowner.

Where was she?

"Oh, this is just great!" said Suzy. "Where'd she go?"

We looked around the room for any sign that Tingledowner had made it back with us. We looked behind her dresser and under the nightstand. Antoine opened the door and let in a flood of sunlight.

He looked across the grassy field and saw nothing.

Suzy sat down on the bed and began to cry. The key was still in her hand and we could still get back. But getting back would be no use if Tingledowner wasn't around to tell us where Jenny was.

"Where'd she go?" Suzy sobbed. "She was supposed to help us!"

"I don't know," said Antoine.

I was standing next to the bed and felt something tug at my shoe lace. I looked down and saw a hand coming up from underneath the bed.

"Guys, I think she's under there," I pointed.

"Boo!" yelled Tingledowner as she jumped out from her hiding spot. "I got you, didn't I, didn't I?"

"What in the world happened to you?" Suzy said. I was wondering the same thing myself, for Tingledowner was no longer Tingledowner. She was Suzy Flannery once again, eight year old Suzy Flannery.

"Do you guys want to see my dolls?" she asked. "I've got three of them, but I have to hide them so nobody can take them from me."

"No," Suzy said, "I don't want to see your dolls. You said you were going to tell us where Jenny was."

"I don't have a Jenny," said Tingledowner, "I have a Peaches, a Lucy, and a Devindra!"

"No," said Suzy, "Jenny's my sister. You were going to tell me where they took her!"

"Do you want to go hide in the forest? Maybe we will see Joseph. He's so nice. You'll love Joey. He lets me call him Joey."

"What's happening?" Suzy asked Antoine.

"I don't know," said Antoine. "Do you still have the key?"

"Yes."

"We need to go back," he said.

"How are we going to find Jenny?" said Suzy. "She was supposed to tell us where she is."

"I know," said Antoine, trying to calm Suzy down.

"That's not going to happen now. We have to go back and try to figure out where they took her."

"I just want this to be over," she said.

"Me too," said Antoine.

Suzy put out her hand and we each grabbed hold of the key and were once again under Shelman's desk, the voice of eight year old Suzy Flannery ringing in our ears.

COBY COLLINS
AND THE
TUNNELS OF
MARLEY

MARLEY ELEMENTARY
ADVENTURES
VOLUME FOUR

JUSTIN
JOHNSON

CONTENTS

PROLOGUE

The three of us stood there, staring at Tingledowner, in disbelief. This woman, who just last year had started my life on this nightmare, and who just yesterday was chasing me around, trying to kill me, was now so sweet and innocent.

"What do you mean you want to go back?" Suzy asked.

"Precisely that," Tingledowner said, "I know one of you must have the key. I wish to go back home."

"Why should we help you?" Antoine piped up. "You started all of this for us."

"That's right," Tingledowner said, "I did. And I can help you end it."

"How?" asked Suzy.

"Easy," said Tingledowner, "I can tell you where your sister is."

"Okay," Suzy said cooly, "where is she?"

"Not so fast," said Tingledowner, reaching her hand out for the key.

Suzy pulled the key, wrapped in Kleenex from her pocket and started to hand it over. Tingledowner's hand was just about to touch the key, when Suzy pulled it back.

"Tell me where Jenny is first."

"No."

"Why not?"

"Because," Tingledowner said, "if I tell you where she is, you may never give me the key."

"Okay, well what do you suggest we do?"

"You come back with me," said Tingledowner. "Once I'm back, I'll tell you about Jenny and you can have the key. I won't need it with Charlotte and papa here. There will be no way anyone can see my diary."

"That sounds reasonable," I said.

Suzy was not so sure. She looked at Tingledowner and then at the key.

"Come on Suzy," Antoine urged, "it's the only way."

"Alright," Suzy said, "but you'd better tell me where she is when we get there."

"I promise," Tingledowner said as a smile came over her face.

Suzy held out her hand, the tissue unwrapped and the key laying on top. All four of us gathered around and counted to three, touched it and were on our way.

*****

We all fell hard on the wooden floor of the cabin. Suzy, Antoine and I stood up and looked around for a sign of Tingeldowner.

Where was she?

"Oh, this is just great!" said Suzy. "Where'd she go?"

We looked around the room for any sign that Tingledowner had made it back with us. We looked behind her dresser and under the nightstand. Antoine opened the door and let in a flood of sunlight.

He looked across the grassy field and saw nothing.

Suzy sat down on the bed and began to cry. The key was still in her hand and we could still get back. But getting back would be no use if Tingledowner wasn't around to tell us where Jenny was.

"Where'd she go?" Suzy sobbed. "She was supposed to help us!"

"I don't know," said Antoine.

I was standing next to the bed and felt something tug at my shoe lace. I looked down and saw a hand coming up from underneath the bed.

"Guys, I think she's under there," I pointed.

"Boo!" yelled Tingledowner as she jumped out from her hiding spot. "I got you, didn't I, didn't I?"

"What in the world happened to you?" Suzy said.

I was wondering the same thing myself, for Tingledowner was no longer Tingledowner. She was Suzy Flannery once again, eight year old Suzy Flannery.

"Do you guys want to see my dolls?" she asked. "I've got three of them, but I have to hide them so nobody can take them from me."

"No," Suzy said, "I don't want to see your dolls. You said you were going to tell us where Jenny was."

"I don't have a Jenny," said Tingledowner, "I have a Peaches, a Lucy, and a Devindra!"

"No," said Suzy, "Jenny's my sister. You were going to tell me where they took her!"

"Do you want to go hide in the forest? Maybe we will see Joseph. He's so nice. You'll love Joey. He lets me call him Joey."

"What's happening?" Suzy asked Antoine.

"I don't know," said Antoine. "Do you still have the key?"

"Yes."

"We need to go back," he said.

"How are we going to find Jenny?" said Suzy. "She was supposed to tell us where she is."

"I know," said Antoine, trying to calm Suzy down. "That's not going to happen now. We have to go back and try to figure out where they took her."

"I just want this to be over," she said.

"Me too," said Antoine.

Suzy put out her hand and we each grabbed hold of the key and were once again under Shelman's desk, the voice of eight year old Suzy Flannery ringing in our ears.

FORMULATE A PLOT

Suzy sobbed. She was inconsolable.

"What did we just do?" Antoine said as he shot up from Shelman's office floor. "What are they playing at? What do they want us to do?"

"I don't know," I said, standing up.

I walked over to the window and looked outside. It was dusk. It would be dark soon and we were no closer to getting Jenny back than we were a few hours ago. We'd gone through all of that for nothing.

Antoine was rifling through Shelman's desk, trying to find something - anything - that would get us closer to Jenny.

"Where'd you leave it?" he muttered to himself. "Where'd you hide it?"

He went through drawer after drawer of files and papers, tossing them right onto the floor. Suzy was still under the desk. As the papers fell she kicked them away, never taking her head out of her folded arms.

I returned my gaze to the window, and out toward the parking lot. There were two cars. My focus was interrupted when I heard two voices.

"That went well enough," I heard Shelman say. I could tell he was walking up the sidewalk, but he was still behind some bushes.

"Well, um, I think, um, you're underestimating the number of our brethren who, um, don't want the Trudell girl to be Converted," Zenu returned.

They came into view now and Shelman stopped and looked up into Zenu's eyes.

"I don't really care. You see, Zenu, my good friend...once it's done, it's done. This position has taught me a great deal about our 'brethren' as you so kindly put it. They are sheep, Zenu. Sheep. And they are just waiting for someone sure and strong to lead them where they need to go. You see, they may say they don't agree, but when the right leader comes along - they follow. That leader is me...and they will follow."

With that, Shelman shook Zenu's hand and walked toward one of the two parked cars. Zenu followed, walking toward the other.

I turned back toward Antoine.

"Found anything?" I asked.

"Nothing."

"Suzy?" I said.

Loud sobs came from below Shelman's desk.

"Come on, Suzy, let's get out of there."

She didn't move.

I looked back at Antoine, "Okay," I said. "Let's discuss our options."

"We could tell our parents and have them call the police," he said.

"That won't work. I tried telling my parents what happened after I touched the hex bolt and they didn't believe me."

"If only we knew where she was," Antoine said, "then we could just worry about how to get her."

"Do you remember what Shelman told Suzy in the gym?"

Antoine scratched his head and furled his eyebrows. "No, I can't remember."

"He said that Jenny wasn't in Marley. That she was being held in some other place."

"Oh yeah," said Antoine. "So what does that mean?"

"I think it's clear," Suzy said, finally emerging from the desk, "don't you?"

I locked eyes with Antoine. We gave each other knowing stares and reluctantly nodded our heads.

"We have to leave Marley," I said.

*****

The thought took a few moments to sink in. We'd actually have to leave Marley. I had never been outside of Marley and I was pretty sure Antoine hadn't either. I wasn't sure about Suzy.

"How are we going to do this?" I asked.

"I don't know," said Suzy.

We stood around Shelman's desk thinking, trying to figure out how to get out of Marley without getting caught.

"We could take a bus," said Antoine after a minute or two.

"I don't have any money," I said turning toward Suzy, "do you?"

"No," she replied.

"Yeah," Antoine said, "me neither."

A few more minutes went by.

"What about the tunnels?" I asked.

"You mean the ones they're filling in with cement?" Suzy asked.

"Yeah," I said. "They've only filled some of them so far. I bet if we wanted to we could take them right out of Marley and to where they've hidden Jenny."

"That sounds like a plan," Antoine said.

"I'm in!" said Suzy, suddenly sounding hopeful.

Suzy cleared Shelman's desk and then put three sheets of paper down. She handed Antoine and me pens.

"Write these items down," she said. "Flashlight, map, clean clothes, batteries and water."

We finished our lists and then Antoine asked, "How are we going to get all of these?"

"We have to go home," she said, "and then meet back up. It's the only way to do this, as much as I hate to say it."

Antoine walked back over to the window in Shelman's office. He looked down along the edge of the building.

"It's gone," he said, shaking his head. "The ladder's gone. How are we going to access the tunnels once we've gone home to pack?"

Another few minutes of silence - and then it dawned on me.

"Meet at my house," I said. "Last year, when we thought we'd defeated them, Antoine and I were chased to my house. We made our escape by climbing up into the bathroom. My parents thought everything was over and got a note from the school saying those tunnels would be closed, so they didn't bother to do anything with the floor. Meet at my house and we'll get into the tunnels that way."

"Sounds good," Suzy said.

"I agree," said Antoine.

"Great," I said, "See you at my house in an hour."

It took us a second to realize that we would actually have to find a way to get out of the school before we could attempt to get anything on our lists.

We looked around and tried the door to Shelman's office, but he'd locked us in. It was probably better that way, because with the extra security measures the school had put in place, we'd probably have set the alarms off trying to leave through the front door. In the end there was only one way out.

The window.

With no ladder.

This was not going to be fun.

PREPARATIONS

I limped up front steps of my house. The fall from the window wasn't as bad as it could have been, but it certainly smarted enough.

I was trying to figure out what I was going to say to my parents. It'd been a day and half since I was home last. They must've been worried.

The door was locked.

This was odd. The sun was starting to go down. Except for nights when there was a birthday to celebrate, or a weekend camping trip, my parents were always home at night.

I reached into my pocket and pulled out my house key, put it in the front door lock and turned. The lock clicked and I opened the door and went inside.

"Mom," I yelled, "Dad?"

No answer.

"Mom?" I yelled again.

No answer.

"Dad?"

I walked into the kitchen. Surely I'd find them sitting at the table waiting in silence for me - and then they'd let me have it!

I slowly pushed the swinging door open and peeked around the edge to discover an empty table.

And then I figured it out. They were in my room. I had to go there next. Where was Jill? And why wasn't she jumping out yelling, "Hey spaz!" or some variation of "You're in trouble?"

"Mom?" I yelled again before approaching the stairs, "Dad?"

I put my hand on the banister and started the climb.

"Jill," I said, "are you up there with mom and dad?"

Still, no answer.

I was half way up the stairs and I could see the bathroom was empty, but the light was on. I just knew they were up here.

When I reached the top of the stairs I made the left hand turn toward my room. The door was open and my sheets were still on the floor from the day before.

That's weird, I thought, *They would normally have picked those up.*

I was starting to get nervous. Something felt really wrong about this, really off. I started tapping on the wall, just to make some noise to let them know that I was on to them. They couldn't fool me that easily.

When I finally peered around the edge of the doorway and into my room I saw that it was exactly as I'd left it the day before - and my parents and sister were not sitting on the bed waiting to pounce.

I couldn't spend too much time worrying about where they were. I had to pack a bag and meet Suzy and Antoine soon. I looked at my alarm clock and realized they would be coming soon. Time to get busy and pack up.

My favorite bag was in my closet. It was big, so it could hold a ton of stuff, plus the straps were thick and padded, so my shoulders wouldn't hurt if I had to fill it.

I opened my closet and and found my trusty flashlight. In the bag it went. Then I went to my dresser and packed some underwear, a few clean shirts, socks and some shorts. I ran downstairs looking for batteries for the flashlight, but couldn't find any.

An unopened gallon of water was still in the pantry, where my mom had put it a few months ago after getting groceries. I'd asked her why we would need a gallon of water to keep in the pantry when we have water from the tap. She'd told me it was for emergencies...and so, here I was, taking it, for an emergency.

I ran back upstairs and checked my room for any other items I thought might be valuable. And then I saw it.

Last year, Antoine had wanted me to be a Fleshbot fan so badly that he bought me a comic book. I'd never read it. It had just sat on my desk for the last year, collecting dust. But now it stood out, like never before.

Wiping the dust from the cover, I picked it up and looked hard at the picture on the front of it. Shivers went through my spine as I saw a Fleshbot's red eyes and strong hand gripping the wrist of a small man and dragging him down a dimly lit corridor.

I flipped through a few pages and was astonished to see Tingledowner, Giga and Flannery in their comic strip boxes. They were talking to each other about a new Convert, one that they were very happy to have acquired. And then on the next page, Shelman was discussing the acquisition with Zenu.

Wait a minute! The man on the cover, the one in their grasps...was he the new Convert?

I turned back to the cover and then frantically started turning through the pages. This man looked familiar. This was about Fred, the man from the meeting in the gym. He'd been dragged out for disagreeing with Shelman, and here he was on the cover of my book, with a story about his capture and Conversion.

The doorbell rang and I knew either Suzy or Antoine was at the door. I rolled the comic book up and stuffed it in my bag before heading downstairs.

When I answered the door, both Suzy and Antoine were standing there, backpacks at the ready.

"Are you all set?" Antoine asked.

"Yes," I answered.

"You don't look so good," he said, "It's like you've seen a ghost. Are you okay?"

"Fine," I said.

"Let's do this," Suzy said, pushing past me. "Where's this door we're going through?"

Antoine and I showed Suzy where the bathroom was. The door was still there. I never used this bathroom anymore. I used to use it all the time, but since that day...well, I go upstairs now.

We opened the door and looked down. The rope ladder was still in tact. Fluorescent lights flooded the tunnels and I could see the singed outline of Flannery, Tingledowner, and Giga from their fall and supposed 'death by water.'

I swallowed hard.

"Are you ready for this?" Antoine asked.

"I'm not so sure," I said, "but it's what we've got to do."

Suzy began climbing down the ladder, then stopped about three steps down. She looked up.

"No matter what happens down here," she said, "I just want to thank you guys for helping me and my sister."

Antoine and I nodded.

And then we began our descent.

TUNNEL

"Which way do we go?" Suzy asked as she touched down.

The tunnel looked to be open in both directions.

"They've already filled most of those tunnels," I said, pointing in the direction of the school. "I think the only way to go is out toward the east side of Marley and take our chances."

"Where will that lead?" she asked.

"I don't know," I said.

Antoine already had his map out and was looking for towns that bordered the east side of Marley.

"There's three towns here, but I don't know which one we'll end up in."

"What are they?" Suzy asked.

"There's Fosterville - that's to the north...then Omeretta - that's in the middle, and," he said, tracing a path from north to south with his finger on the map, "Portentia to the south."

"Well, it'll be one of those, but for right now, it looks like the tunnel only goes in one direction," I said.

Antoine put his map back into his bag and we began to walk.

It was brighter down here then I'd remembered. It's funny the things you don't notice when you're running for your life. Apparently the brightness of the tunnels was one of them.

As we walked I noticed myself becoming colder. There was a dampness down here that I hadn't been prepared for.

The fluorescent lights were in place for about half a mile, as were the rope ladders and doors into houses. But as soon as the doors and ladders stopped - so did the lights.

"You guys brought your flashlights, right?" asked Suzy, as she pulled out a heavy duty, industrial strength camping lantern.

"Yeah," I said. I pulled out my standard, run-of-the-mill, what if the power goes out, flashlight. I turned it on and it flickered a little. "This could be iffy. I couldn't find any batteries."

"It's okay," Antoine said, "I couldn't find a flashlight, but I did get these." He reached into his bag and brought out four very small batteries.

I looked at my flashlight, and then back to the batteries. I turned my flashlight off and unscrewed the cap, pulled out one of the batteries and placed it in Antoine's hand to compare the two. They were not the same size.

"Great," exclaimed Suzy. "You guys have one flashlight and no batteries between the two of you. This is not exactly what I'd call prepared."

"Well, I'm s-o-o-o-rry," Antoine shot back. "Flashlight batteries aren't exactly something I use everyday. In fact, today might be the first time in my life that I've ever used them."

"Alright," said Suzy apologetically. "I should've been nicer about that."

"It's okay."

I put the battery back into my flashlight and turned it on. It flickered, like before, but it worked.

We started walking. It became apparent that Suzy's lantern was the way to go. It was bright and strong and lit the way just perfectly. My flashlight lasted a few hundred feet then went dead.

"We'll be okay," Suzy reassured us, "as long as we have the lantern."

The deeper we walked into the tunnels the more signs of life we began to see. Though, these were not the signs of life we were hoping for. Snakes started to emerge from little puddles that had collected from water that had dripped from the ceiling.

"Are those poisonous?" Antoine asked.

"I don't know," I said.

"I hope not," Suzy said, trying to stay positive. "It doesn't really matter anyway."

"What do you mean," I asked.

"What I mean is, we're all this way from home and on a mission to get Jenny. There's no turning back, whether they're poisonous or not."

She had a point. I didn't like the point, but I did have to admit that she had one.

"Just try not to get bitten," she advised.

"Thanks for the tip," said Antoine in a snarky tone.

After that we walked in silence for a long time, Suzy's lantern brightly lighting the way, as the occasional snake slithered in and out of our path.

I had time to think down here. It was strange, but it felt like I was alone, even though Suzy and Antoine were with me. They didn't say much and the dripping water and slithering snakes made it easy to forget they were near.

I started to think about my parents. Where were they? Were they looking for me, or were they just going on with life as usual? Had Antoine and Suzy's parents been home to greet them, and if so, why would they allow them to leave the house again to chase after these Fleshbots? I thought about Suzy and how desperate she must be feeling to find Jenny...and how if that were me, I don't know if I'd be strong enough to continue. And then I thought about Jill, and something I'd heard in the gym. Zenu told the crowd that they were hoping to get her, and it wouldn't be too difficult because I was following them.

They've got them.

I kept walking, not saying a word. Just wondering how I could have been so stupid as to think my family was at home playing a trick on me. And then my heart leapt into my throat and I began to sweat profusely.

"Guys," I said frantically, "were your parents home when you went to get your bags and stuff?"

"No," said Antoine.

"Mine neither," said Suzy.

I just came out with it. "They've got them!"

"What? No way Coby, that's crazy," argued Antoine.

"Is it?" I shot back. "All three of us were gone for a day and a half and we go back to our houses to get some supplies, so that we can be gone a lot longer than that, and none of our parents are home. And Zenu and Shelman were telling the other Fleshbots just a few hours ago that by taking Jenny they would have the opportunity to Convert more than just her. Oh, and by the way, they don't just take kids. Remember in Tingledowner's diary how her father, a grown man, had gone into town a human and come back a Fleshbot? They've got them, Antoine. They've got them all."

I had just enough time to read the expression on Antoine's face that said he believed me, before a huge rat ran in front of Suzy.

She screamed.

The lantern slipped.

Broken glass.

Darkness.

HEAR THAT?

I don't know how long we sat there in the darkness. It seemed like forever. But it would have wouldn't it? We now knew there were rats down here and we could hear them squeak. We could hear their claws tapping along the cement floor and we could occasionally feel them brush past our shoes.

We also knew there were snakes. And in the darkness our sense of hearing became much keener, much more aware. We could hear them slither in and out of the puddles and along the edges of the walls. I could feel them sliding past me, taking every opportunity to rub up against my ankle and remind me we were not alone.

And along with all this, we were left in the dark with the thought that our families were in the process of being Converted into Fleshbots. Each one of us feeling alone and afraid, by ourselves, with our thoughts, in the middle of the blackness.

"Are you guys okay?" Antoine asked.

"Yeah, I'm okay," I returned.

Suzy didn't respond with words, but instead broke down sobbing.

I reached to console her, to let her know that it wasn't her fault, but I couldn't see and my arm touched nothing before I felt it come back to my chest.

"It's gonna be okay," I said, hoping she would at least hear my words.

"Yeah, Suzy," Antoine jumped in, "It's no big deal. We'll just try to feel our way along and hope we find our way out of here."

This didn't exactly help as much as Antoine hoped it would. Suzy began crying even harder, if that was possible.

"Come on guys," I said, "find the walls and walk in the direction we were going before. Ignore the snakes and rats, they're not going to hurt us anyway."

"How can you be so sure?" Suzy asked between sobs.

"I can't," I answered, "but we might as well be moving forward when they do get us."

"That's great, Coby," said Antoine, "way to make her feel better."

I ignored this and started moving forward. The truth was, there was no way to make her feel better. This was a lousy situation we found ourselves in. But it was important to keep moving forward. There was more at stake than a few rats and snakes climbing on us. This was about our families. All of them. It was time to go get them and return them to safety. I wasn't sure how we were going to do it, but standing still in the dark was definitely not it.

I wasn't sure how far we'd walked when we heard it. It was a noise, steps coming from in front of us. We could hear heavy breathing, panting, like they'd been running, followed by silence.

I stopped and felt that Suzy and Antoine had stopped a few feet behind me.

"You guys hear that?" I whispered.

FRED

The noised continued to get closer. "Hello," it said in a tentative voice. "Hello?"

The steps and calls came closer and closer. And within a few moments we could see a light. Not a flashlight, or a lantern like we had, but fire.

The inconsistent glow was bouncing off the wall as it came toward us. We could start to see that we were about to hit a dead end and then the tunnel veered south. The glow kept coming.

We stood still and as I looked back I could start to see Suzy and Antoine. The light from the fire allowed me to see their eyes, glassy and full of fear. Tears were shining on Suzy's face. And, though Antoine would never admit it, he'd been doing a fair share of crying as well.

The calls became louder and softer all at the same time. They were getting closer, but they were becoming fainter, like they might quit altogether. Who ever was on the other end of this corner was clearly close.

Within seconds, light from the fire filled the once black cavern we'd been in. It blinded us. I put my hands up to my face to shield my eyes from the brightness.

"Kids?" the voice asked. "What are you doing down here?"

"Mr.," I said, "We can't see you. Could you please put the light down?"

"Oh yeah," he said, "sure."

He brought the torch down to his side and allowed us to see him for the first time.

"You!" Suzy Screamed.

She started to run in the opposite direction. She had reason to, for standing in front of us now, was the Fleshbot named Fred. We'd seen him dragged out of the meeting in the gym.

"Wait, no!" shouted the man, "I won't hurt you, I promise. I'm not one of them anymore. I'm human, just like you."

"Prove it," Antoine said. "Show us your hand."

The man held out his hand for Antoine to examine. He looked closely and determined that Fred was telling the truth. There were no bolts or screws or anything like that.

"You're Fred," I said. "You're the one who stood up to Shelman."

"Yes."

"But you were..."

"Dead," he said.

"Yeah," I said. "We saw you get thrown into the hallway after you did what you did. It looked like you were as good as gone."

"I thought the same thing myself," he said.

"Wait a minute," Suzy said, "what happened to you then?"

"I'm not really sure, exactly," answered Fred, shrugging his shoulders. "All I know is that when I finally came to, I was down here with this torch."

"So, what are you doing now? Where are you going?" Antoine asked.

"I'm on my way to save that little Trudell girl?"

"That's my sister," Suzy said through gritted teeth.

"That's your sister? Such a terrible thing they're trying to do to her."

"Yeah," I said.

"Do you know where she is?" Suzy jumped in.

"Kind of," Fred said. "We were all told which town they'd put her in, but we weren't given any particulars."

"So, which town is she in?" Suzy asked. I wanted to tell her to give this man a break. She was a little abrasive, but I understood.

"She's in Bale," Fred said. "It's about 10 miles in the other direction. You guys have been going the wrong way."

"What do you mean, the wrong way?" Suzy asked.

"Yeah," I said, "we can't go the other way, they've blocked the tunnels."

Fred nodded his head and shook his finger in the air.

"Shelman is very smart," he said. "He would sacrifice a section of the tunnel to make people believe that all was right with their world."

"You mean he filled in the tunnel to fool us?" Antoine asked.

I felt so stupid. Of course he did. It's perfect. By getting us to believe that those tunnels were closed, he forced us in the complete opposite direction. It was genius.

Fred nodded and pointed in the direction we'd just come from.

"That's the way you've got to go," he said. "If you want to find the Trudell girl, anyway."

I looked at Antoine and Suzy, the thought suddenly occurring to me that this could be another one of Shelman's tricks. He could have staged the whole thing with Fred, knowing that we were there. Knowing that we'd see him thrown out of the gym, and knowing that we would eventually end up down here, face to face.

I could tell by the looks on their faces that the same thoughts were racing through their heads as well.

"What do you guys think, can we trust him?" I asked. I just came out with it. It may have been rude, but this was not exactly the best time in the world be worrying about manners.

"I don't know," said Antoine.

"Yeah," Suzy chimed in, "I'm not so sure we should."

"It's okay," Fred said, "I'm not one of them. In fact, I'm on the other side now. I'm on my way to Bale to help the Trudell girl, and join up with..."

His voice trailed off, as though he thought he may have said too much.

"With whom?" Suzy asked, pressing Fred and leaning in.

"Nevermind," Fred said. "The bottom line is this - I am no longer a Fleshbot. When those men took care of me in the gymnasium, they made sure of that. All I want to do is help your sister and free her from the grips of an evil machine. I'm heading to Bale, because, last I knew, that's where she was being kept. If you want to come with me you may. If you want to go the direction you started, foolish as it may be, you may do that also."

I looked into his eyes. I couldn't put my finger on it, but I had a good feeling about this man, Fred, and what he was trying to do. He'd stood up to Shelman and taken the fall for it. He was an example to Fleshbots. He was Shelman's poster boy for what not to do, and that sat right with me. I didn't know what Antoine and Suzy were thinking, but I was thinking Fred was going to lead us to the right place. He would take us where we needed to go.

"I'm going with Fred," I announced.

"Me too," said Antoine, nodding.

We looked toward Suzy, waiting for her decision. She looked at us, then she looked at him. It was clear that she was not in the frame of mind to make the most rational decision. The thought of going it alone was more than likely the deciding factor in her choosing to turn around and go with us to Bale. For she did not sound sure of herself, or of anything, when she uttered the word, "okay." But that didn't really matter now.

What mattered was that we were sticking together, right or wrong. And, if we were right, we would have one of the best people to help us out - A man, who'd been a Fleshbot five hours earlier, and who, because he no longer believed in what they were doing, was relieved of his powers and sent down to the tunnels like a rat. He was on our side now.

Fred was our leader...and we would follow him to Bale.

TO BALE

We began walking in the other direction.

"So," I said, "when we get to the school, how're we going to get past the cement?"

"That's easy," Fred said. "We'll simply climb the last ladder before the cement, walk to the other side of the school and climb that ladder down, and then be on our way."

It sounded easy enough.

"Shelman didn't have any intention of filling in the whole tunnel system," Fred said. "He simply wanted to give the illusion that he cared about what happened to Marley."

We walked along for a few minutes. Nobody spoke. The glow of Fred's torch illuminated the corridor enough for us to see where we going. Rats and snakes scurried as the light revealed them.

After a few moments, Suzy started asking questions.

"What are we going to find in Bale?"

"I don't know exactly," said Fred. "I was told the Trudell girl was there."

"Her name is Jenny," Suzy informed him.

"Sorry," Fred said, "We've just been calling her the Trudell girl."

There was something in his voice that made it apparent he had no intention of ever calling her Jenny.

"So," Suzy continued, "where do you think Jenny is?"

"I don't know exactly," said Fred. "I was told she was there, and I know a few of the others are going to be there too. I just have to get there to meet them."

"*Others?*" Suzy asked.

"Yes. I was a member of the opposition. We stood up against The Four on a number of major issues. This thing with the Trudell girl was the latest issue we were taking on. The idea that any member of the Fleshbot Legion would be willing to Convert a child so young..." his eyes looked off in the distance like he was searching for the right word, but he never completed his thought.

"So you're leading us to other Fleshbots?" Suzy pressed.

I looked at Antoine with up turned eyebrows. Was this really where we wanted to go?

He returned my glance and I could see the trepidation in his eyes.

"Well," Fred continued, "if that's how you prefer to look at it. I call them my friends, and the Trudell girl is your sister, so..."

His voice trailed off again.

At this point, our options were limited and we all knew it. We continued to follow Fred in silence.

After about an hour or so, we reached the cement wall that had been poured at the school. Fred told us to climb the ladder just before it.

"We'll walk to the other end of the school and go back underground. It should be a straight shot to Bale from there," he said.

We walked silently, the burning flame of Fred's torch and the soles of our shoes on the floor were the only sounds.

I was feeling numb. I just wanted this to be over, but a part of me knew this was far from over. There were so many questions that were yet to be answered. How were we going to find Jenny? Were our families involved in this now? And, perhaps, the biggest question of all - Was it safe to follow Fred?

When we arrived at the far end of the school, Fred stopped. He looked around for a minute, like he wasn't sure what he was doing or what he was looking for. And then he made a quick move toward an unmarked door under a stairwell.

"It took me a minute," he said. "I've only been here a handful of times and I couldn't quite remember where the door was."

Suzy, Antoine and I stood back and gave Fred some space as he opened the first door and then swung the 'door in the floor' up and rested it against the cinder block wall.

"Are you coming?" he asked.

Looking at Suzy and Antoine, I could tell they weren't sure. I definitely wasn't sure, but someone had to make the first move. In a way, I thought it had to be me. I was the one who got us into this mess last year with Tingledowner. I was going to have to be the one to take this step and try to get us out of it.

I stepped forward and said, "I'm coming."

Fred nodded.

Suzy stepped forward next.

"Me too."

The three of us looked at Antoine, waiting for him to make his choice.

"Alright," he sighed, hanging his head as he stepped in our direction.

Fred was the first to go down the ladder. I let Suzy and Antoine go next. I'll save you the details of how I managed. I'm sure you can already guess, it wasn't pretty.

The torch illuminated the tunnels once again. We followed Fred away from the school and into uncharted territory. It was scary to have no idea what would greet us on our journey, or if we would even complete our journey.

It didn't matter now, though. We were on our way to Bale.

DEFEATABLE

We walked for what seemed like an hour or more. As we went farther away from the school, the tunnel grew darker and the rats and snakes became more prevalent.

They scurried every which way and seemed undeterred by Fred's torch or the sounds of our feet. They came close to us, and at times it seemed as though they would crawl right up our legs if we'd let them.

I started to feel oddly itchy all over. It was that feeling you get when you just know something is on you. Like a bug is crawling up your skin.

It was Suzy who broke the silence.

"So, when we get to Bale, what's going to happen?"

"I don't know exactly," said Fred, "but it's going to be big."

"What do you mean?"

"The Fleshbot Legion has been at odds for quite sometime," Fred began. "It's probably safe to say that there never was a 'golden' period for them. They've always been divided on certain issues. It's always led to threats of uprisings and the possibility of overthrowing those in power. But this time..."

Fred let this thought trail off, like he'd done before. Suzy made sure he finished this one.

"What's going on this time?"

"Oh, right," he stammered, seemingly trying to remember what he'd just said. "Well, this time I think the uprising may really happen. Shelman and Flannery have really upset the Legion with this Conversion of the Trudell girl. And somehow they got Zenu to go along with it."

"I'm not sure I understand," I piped up. "What do you *think* is going to happen in Bale?"

Fred stopped. He turned toward me and moved the torch across his face, giving me a clear and disturbing view of his eyes. They were focused, like he was looking through me.

"When we get to Bale, it will be an all out war. We've been preparing for months and now it will finally come to be. Two sides in and only one will come out."

"What do you mean? Aren't you guys...I mean, aren't Fleshbots unbeatable?"

"That's what they'd have you believe, isn't it?" he said with a chuckle. "But in all actuality we are very much beatable. You saw what they did to me, right?"

It was true. Fred had been a Fleshbot just hours ago and now he was walking with us in the tunnel - a human.

"Alright," Suzy stepped up, "how do you do it?"

"It's actually rather easy," Fred said. "You see, each Fleshbot has a life cord. It's like a cord that gets plugged into a wall outlet. But in the case of a Fleshbot, it gets plugged into the back where their power box is located. When that cord is cut or removed from the Fleshbot, he collapses and the robot within dies."

"So how did you come back?" Antoine asked.

"I was just Converted a few years ago. Once the robot within dies, the human can re-emerge and come back to life. If however, the person coming back is too old, they will simply wither away and become part of the earth."

"Flannery?" I thought out loud.

"Exactly," Fred smiled. "All three of them - Shelman, Flannery and Zenu. They were all Converted over a hundred years ago. That's how they've come to be so powerful - longevity. And once their power cord is severed, they will be no more. They are the head of the beast. Remove the head and the body will fall. If we defeat them, it's over. Getting to them will be the hard part. They're well protected."

"So, how many do you think there are on our side?" Suzy asked.

"Not as many as they have," Fred said. "That's the challenge. We're outnumbered five to one. We're going to have to figure out a way to get to the head before the body takes us all out."

He let out a quick sigh and then moved the torch across his face once more. He turned and began walking in the direction we'd been going, this time with purpose in his steps. He was on a mission. And no one - not even the Fleshbot Legion - was going to stop him.

FRED'S STORY

"Can we stop and take a break?" I panted.

Fred had been walking much faster than before. That, plus the two days with no sleep and very little food was starting to make me weak.

"No," Fred grunted.

We walked a few more steps and then Suzy came to my rescue.

"We need to sit down, even if it's just for a few minutes. I have granola bars in my bag and there's enough for all of us."

Fred stopped and turned around. He looked from Antoine to Suzy to me. I'm pretty sure he was trying to think of a good reason why he shouldn't just leave us there.

Ultimately, he couldn't come up with one. That's one thing about humans. They are much more compassionate than Fleshbots.

"Fine," he said begrudgingly. "You get five minutes. After that, we're on the move."

"Thank you so much," I said.

We all sat down, even Fred. He placed his torch in a crack in the cement and let it stand on its own, illuminating us while we ate.

Suzy gave us each a granola bar and some gummy snacks.

"How much longer until we get to Bale?" Antoine asked.

"Not long now," said Fred. "We should be there in less than an hour...as long as you don't have to sit down again." He looked at me as he said this. I looked away and continued to eat. I devoured my food so quickly, barely chewing it before it was catapulted down my throat.

After a few minutes Fred looked at his watch.

"Time to go," he said getting to his feet and picking up the torch.

He didn't even wait for Suzy to zip up her back pack or Antoine to stuff the wrappers in his pocket. The light from the torch was moving steadily away from us and we had to rush to catch up.

Most of the next hour passed slowly. It seemed to take forever to get to Bale.

We had more run ins with snakes and rats, and the dampness of the tunnels really started to set in. But worse than all that was the fact that nobody spoke a word. We were all on this path, walking together, and yet, we were very much alone.

I thought about my parents and my sister. I wondered if I would find them in Bale. I wondered about Suzy's sister, Jenny, and what her fate would be. And if my parents were there, were Suzy's and Antoine's as well?

Not to mention the fact that we didn't really know where we going, or what would be there when we arrived. I mean, Fred seemed like he was a human now. He seemed like he was on our side, but I'd been duped before...I didn't want to be duped again. Were we headed for a Fleshbot ambush? Was this journey going to be our last? Was that crummy granola bar and those stupid gummy snacks going to be the last food I ever tasted?

I didn't want to ask Fred too much. He seemed like his focus was elsewhere. But I couldn't help myself.

"So, what's your story?"

"What do you mean, what's my story?" he said, not bothering to turn in my direction to address me.

"I mean, what...I mean, how...and when...did you..."

"Become a Fleshbot?"

"Yeah," I said feeling a little embarrassed that I'd brought it up.

"I was working in Grendale. I was a janitor at the local school and a man named Jeffery Wommat was my boss. He took an interest in me and said he liked what I was doing, liked my work ethic.

"One day, he called me to his office and said he had an offer for me. He asked me if I'd like to live forever and have powers far beyond my wildest dreams. Well, that was it. I took one look at my dry, dirt caked hands and my sweat soaked shirt and said 'Absolutely, sir'. He Converted me right then and there.

"Things went well for a while, but then I started to question what was going on with the Legion and their policies. The more Fleshbots I met, and the more gatherings I was asked to be a part of, the more I realized that maybe I'd chosen wrong. At the time, I couldn't imagine anything worse than what I was doing - cleaning up after kids for a living. But there's always something worse. Sometimes you don't have it nearly as bad as you think you do. And it didn't take me long to realize I was part of the problem.

"So, I started speaking out. At first, I'd talk with Fleshbots who'd already made their opinions known. I knew who I could safely vent my frustrations to. I also knew when to keep my mouth shut and do what I was told. It was hard, living this double life - but it's what I had to do to survive...or so I thought.

"Eventually, I decided it wasn't worth it. It's funny, but even though I was a robot, I never lost my ability to feel. I saw a lot of things that I couldn't ignore. Things that filled me with a sorrow so deep it was unbearable. And no matter how much I tried to keep it bottled up inside, I couldn't. I began speaking out. Every chance I got, to anyone who would listen. The problem was, they weren't in any position to do anything - and most of them didn't care anyway. I knew the Legion was headed in a bad direction. Every move they made seemed to move one step closer to this deplorable place we're in now.

"Of course, not everyone thinks it's a bad place to be. Shelman, Flannery and Zenu are quite happy with the Legion they've created. But I knew what they were doing and I knew I didn't agree with it. And this thing with..."

Fred stopped and took a moment to look at Suzy. The light from the torch hit Fred's face at just the right angle and I could see his cheeks glisten with tears.

"Your sister's name is Jenny, right?"

Suzy nodded.

"Yeah," he continued, "this thing with Jenny was the final straw. I couldn't sit back anymore. I was yelling into a void. I knew I had a small faction starting to listen to what I was saying, but not enough for an overthrow of Legion Leaders. I knew I had to do something major to get their attention. And so, I stood up at that meeting and made myself an example. A martyr of sorts.

"I knew the risk wasn't that high. I'd only been a Fleshbot for a few years, so I knew when they took me out of there and pulled my life cord that I would eventually come back as my human self, aged only a little. I also knew that more than half the Fleshbots in that gym were on my side. They were looking for someone to do something, anything.

"And most of them couldn't stand up, like I'd asked them to do. I knew they had to look down. If they gave themselves away in front of Shelman, every last life cord would have been pulled, and most of them would have withered away without a trace that they ever walked this Earth."

Fred stopped suddenly and looked around. He pointed to a ladder that had just become visible, a few feet in front of us.

"We're here."

A NEW DEVELOPMENT

We emerged from the ladder into a room full of hundreds of unknown faces.

I suddenly had a bad feeling about this. Their stares were daggers and lasers pointed right at us.

"What are you doing Fred?" asked a man with red eyes. He was short in stature and normally wouldn't seem so scary, but those red eyes brought back a flood of fear from within me.

"It's okay, Garret," said Fred, putting his hands out to calm him down.

"Explain yourself," Garret fired back.

"I'd like you all to meet the Trudell girl's sister, Suzy," Fred said, making a grand gesture in her direction. "I found them in the tunnels, just outside of Marley. They're here to help."

"Help?" shouted a woman from the back of the room. "How in the world are those *kids* going to help?"

"Listen," said Fred, "I know you weren't expecting me to bring guests, but I did. And these *kids,* as you put it, have more of a vested interest in this than we do. Suzy's sister has been taken and they are here to get her back...no matter what it takes. Welcome them. Embrace them. Take them in as one of our brethren, for tonight, they fight with us!"

That did it. Just like that the place erupted in cheers. Everyone in the room knew that Fred was their leader. They knew that if he trusted us, they should trust us too.

They closed in on us, shaking our hands, giving hugs and introducing themselves at a rapid rate. It was too much to take in.

"To the table!" Fred called, "Get the battle map!"

Just like that, the crowd cleared and a large table came into view. It was the biggest table I'd ever seen. Two burly Fleshbots carried over a gigantic map and placed it in front of Fred.

Fred looked at us and explained that we were deep in the woods outside of Bale. He pointed to our location on the map.

"This cabin is one of four along this clearing," he said. "The other three are full of Fleshbots and former Fleshbots, like us, ready to fight the Legion."

He moved his finger to another section of the map.

"This is Lake Wanya. It's located just behind these cabins. It's our defense plan. If anything should happen to you out there, you just run to the water. Don't worry, it's shallow until about two hundred feet out. They won't be able to hurt you if you're in there."

He moved his finger to the other side of the map.

"This is where they are, in the trees and thicket just in front of the cabins. They know we're here. They also know that we aren't going along with their plan. This has been a recent development - I was only notified of this moments after we arrived."

I swallowed hard.

"So," continued Fred, "this is no longer an uprising - we are going to be attacked. And we must be ready when it happens."

Just as Fred had finished this last thought a voice came ringing through the trees and into the cabin.

"Come out and meet your fate!"

It was Shelman, his voice boomed through a bullhorn.

I looked around the room, noting the look in everyone's eyes. It was a mix of fear and determination. Clearly, this was happening far sooner than they were ready for. But it was here and they would have to find the courage to stand up and defend themselves.

"To your knees," Fred commanded.

Everyone dropped to one knee and bowed their heads. Nobody spoke, except Fred.

"This is what we've waited for. It came much sooner than we thought, but we are ready. We will fight tonight with courage and conviction. We will make their wrongs right again. When tonight it over," he paused here and nodded at Suzy, "Jenny goes home to her family, and the Legion is destroyed. Go after their life cords and pull. Help each other out. They are dividers, we are uniters - and tonight we will fight united! It's now or never, are you ready!"

"Yeah!!!" the room erupted once more, louder than before.

"Let's do this!"

LET IT BEGIN

We rushed out into the clearing, joining the other three groups of Fleshbots.

"My, my," said Shelman condescendingly. "There are quite a lot of you, aren't there?"

All at once, the Legion emerged from the trees. They had more than double the man power.

"We have quite a few members on our side as well," laughed Shelman. "More than enough to make sure that when you're all gone, you won't be missed."

Flannery walked over to where Shelman was standing and took the bull horn.

"Is Suzy Trudell down there?"

I tried to grab her hand, but she was out of my reach and rushing to the front of the crowd before I could stop her.

"I'm right here!" she yelled.

"Good," said Flannery nodding. "Show her what she came here for."

A giant light clicked on. It was pointed directly at a tree to Flannery's left.

"Jenny!" Suzy screamed. "Let her go!"

Jenny was chained to the tree and sitting unconscious at its base.

"I'm afraid you stand to lose more than just a sister," he mocked. He turned to a frumpy looking man on his right, "Show her."

The frumpy looking man disappeared into the trees and came back a moment later, guiding two larger figures. It was easy to see that they were tied up. The man led them into the light and deposited them next to Jenny.

"No!" Suzy sobbed, "Let my parents go!"

"Afraid not, dear," said Flannery. "Say, is Antoine down there with you?"

Antoine shot me a fearful glance and then worked his way toward the front of the group. I followed, having a feeling I would be next.

"I'm here," said Antoine.

"Good," Flannery chuckled, "Giga, would you like to do the honors?"

Giga stepped forward with Antoine's parents and pushed them down into the light, just in front of Suzy's family.

Antoine made no plea. He hung his head and began to cry.

I knew what was coming next.

"Coby," Flannery started, "I see you've already worked your way to the front. Either, you wanted to be with your friends when they got their bad news, or you knew that you were next. Which is it?"

I didn't answer. I just watched as Zenu flicked on a light that shone on the tree next to the one Jenny was strapped to. My sister Jill was at the base of this tree, her head hanging limply on her right shoulder. The same man who'd brought Suzy's parents out, now brought out mine. He unceremoniously dumped them at the feet of my sister.

Fred came up behind us.

"It's okay," he said, "we'll get them back."

I felt sick to my stomach. My legs began to tremble and I could feel the tears rush forth.

Shelman's voice came over the bullhorn once again.

"Now that everyone knows what's at stake here, I guess there's only one thing left to do."

He paused and looked around, making sure everyone on his side appeared ready. And then he gave the order.

"Get 'em!"

COBY COLLINS
AND THE
BATTLE
AT BALE

MARLEY ELEMENTARY
ADVENTURES
VOLUME FIVE

JUSTIN
JOHNSON

CONTENTS

PROLOGUE

We rushed out into the clearing, joining the other three groups of Fleshbots.

"My, my," said Shelman condescendingly. "There are quite a lot of you, aren't there?"

All at once, the Legion emerged from the trees. They had more than five times the man power.

"We have quite a few members on our side as well," laughed Shelman. "More than enough to make sure that when you're all gone, you won't be missed."

Flannery walked over to where Shelman was standing and took the bull horn.

"Is Suzy Trudell down there?"

I tried to grab her hand, but she was out of my reach and rushing to the front of the crowd before I could stop her.

"I'm right here!" she yelled.

"Good," said Flannery nodding. "Show her what she came here for."

A giant light clicked on. It was pointed directly at a tree to Flannery's left.

"Jenny!" Suzy screamed. "Let her go!"

Jenny was chained to the tree and sitting unconsciously at its base.

"I'm afraid you stand to lose more than just a sister," he mocked. He turned to a frumpy looking man on his right, "Show her."

The frumpy looking man disappeared into the trees and came back a moment later, guiding two larger figures. It was easy to see that they were tied up. The man led them into the light and deposited them next to Jenny.

"No!" Suzy sobbed, "Let my parents go!"

"Afraid not, dear," said Flannery. "Say, is Antoine down there with you?"

Antoine shot me a fearful glance and then worked his way toward the front of the group. I followed, having a feeling I would be next.

"I'm here," said Antoine.

"Good," Flannery chuckled, "Giga, would you like to do the honors?"

Giga stepped forward with Antoine's parents and pushed them down into the light, just in front of Suzy's family.

Antoine made no plea. He hung his head and began to cry.

I knew what was coming next.

"Coby," Flannery started, "I see you've already worked your way to the front. Either, you wanted to be with your friends when they got their bad news, or you knew that you were next. Which is it?"

I didn't answer. I just watched as Zenu flicked on a light. It shone on the tree next to the one Jenny was strapped to. My sister Jill was at the base of this tree, her head hanging limply on her right shoulder. The same man who'd brought Suzy's parents out, now brought out mine. He unceremoniously dumped them at the feet of my sister.

Fred came up behind us.

"It's okay," he said, "we'll get 'em back."

I felt sick to my stomach. My legs began to tremble and I could feel the tears rush forth.

Shelman's voice came over the bullhorn once again.

"Now that everyone knows what's at stake here, I guess there's only one thing left to do."

He paused and looked around, making sure everyone on his side appeared ready. And then he gave the order.

"Get 'em!"

AND IT BEGINS

Fleshbots on both sides began running toward each other and shouting incoherent war cries. Shelman's group from the woods, running downhill at us. Our side running up to meet them eagerly.

Before I made a move I looked back toward the water. Fred had told us to go there if it looked like things were going to get bad. It took me by surprise how calm the water was. Not a single ripple or wave was coming in or out. The reflection of the moon was perfectly still. I had a feeling I would be disturbing the surface of the water soon enough.

"Cut their life cords!" Fred shouted, running from side to side, trying to give final instructions. "If you can't get a clear shot, just lunge and rip the cords from their power box!"

The few that heard, nodded to show they understood and took up the charge with the rest.

I turned my attention to Suzy and Antoine, who were still standing next to me looking up the hill.

"What do you want to do?" I asked.

"What do you mean?" Suzy answered.

Antoine didn't acknowledge me. He just kept looking up the hill where his parents were sitting, propped up on one another.

"I mean, do we fight? Or do we run for the edge of the water?"

Suzy looked up the hill, "My parents are up there. Your parents are up there. Our sisters are up there...and you want to run?"

"No," I said, "I don't want to run!"

"Alright then," Suzy said. A look of apprehension came across her face for just a second and then it was gone and she was focused. "Let's go do this!"

"Right!"

We were about a quarter of the way up the hill when we looked back and discovered that Antoine hadn't moved.

"I'm going back to get him," I said.

"What are we going to do with him?"

"I don't know, but we can't just let him stand there."

I ran back down toward Antoine. I didn't know what I was going to do. He was in shock. There was no way he was going to snap out of it and fight. Getting him to a safe place was my only option.

Antoine's arm was limp and he offered no resistance when I grabbed him and started to drag him to the edge of the water. He just turned with me and walked behind me.

Then I heard it. Through all of the noise and shouts, this one rang above them all. It was Suzy.

"Coby!"

I turned just in time to see her being dragged away by one of Shelman's grunts. The Fleshbot picked her right up. Her feet were kicking wildly, not hitting anything.

I turned to Antoine. "Listen, I have to go help Suzy, she's in a lot of trouble. Stay here and if one of

274

them comes toward you, jump into the water...do you understand?"

He stood there motionless, staring out across the lake.

I turned to head up the hill in Suzy's direction. She was yelling something else now. I couldn't hear her.

"What?" I shouted.

"Look out!"

It was too late. A sharp pain shot up my arm and I realized I had been captured. I was being dragged up the hill.

He had me by the arm and he was walking much faster than I was capable of. It wasn't long before I lost my balance and fell forward. The Fleshbot did not release his grasp, or give me a chance to get up and recover my dignity. Rather, he grabbed hard and dragged me up the hill. Wet leaves, grass and mud plastered my face on the way.

'Antoine,' I thought. I was able to turn my head just enough to look back and see that Antoine was being led up the hill gently. There was no fight on his end. It might as well have been me leading him up to his doom.

I felt something hit my right arm and realized I had just been slammed into a tree.

"Look this way," the Fleshbot reprimanded, "Or I do it again!"

The pain was really starting to set in now. I looked forward and allowed the leaves and mud to slap my face. It was better than the alternative.

Suzy's screams tore through the air as she was forced toward the trees. She was putting up quite a fight.

And then her screams stopped.

My face parted the sea of mud and leaves for another few hundred feet before I was finally yanked up by my left arm.

"Look at friend," my captor laughed.

I wiped the mud from my eyes with my available arm and looked for Suzy.

In the darkness I could see her lying at the base of a tree. She was motionless. I didn't know how they'd gotten her so quiet.

Then I found out.

I was turned around suddenly so my back faced Suzy. My captor then picked me up and hurled me toward the tree.

I felt a searing pain at the base of my neck as I made contact with the sturdy oak. And then my head snapped back.

And then, nothing.

WHAT IN THE WHAT

Antoine was in such shock and moved so easily that the Fleshbots took pity on him. They shoved him into the mud next to us, but saved him the trauma of being thrust into the tree.

When I finally woke up, I was draped over Suzy's right hip, my face down in the mud and leaves once again. I remained still just in case we were being watched closely.

I could hear the shouting and yelling of the battle raging down in the clearing. It was loud, yet distant.

"Suzy," I whispered, my face still planted firmly in mud.

She didn't answer but I felt her hip move slightly under my legs.

The move must not have been as subtle as I thought, because within a few seconds I was grabbed by the same Fleshbot who'd grabbed me earlier. This time I was placed at the base of the tree next to Antoine. Suzy was placed right next to me while the Fleshbot who'd taken her ran a rope around the perimeter of the tree and tied us into place.

The three Fleshbots stood back and folded their arms across their chests, admiring their handy work.

"Shelman be pleased," mine said.

"Yes," said Suzy's.

Antoine's remained silent and nodded.

In the fading light of a nearby campfire I could see their clothes. They were tattered and torn, nothing more than rags. It was clear by the job that Shelman had them do and the clothes they were wearing, that these Fleshbots were among the lowest in rank.

Suzy was crying on one side of me and Antoine was staring off into space on the other side. And I was putting it all together in the middle.

"So how does it feel to be Shelman's grunts?" I asked.

Suzy stopped crying and snapped her head in my direction.

"What are you doing?"

"It's okay," I whispered. "Just go with it."

I didn't really know what I was doing, but it was worth a shot.

"You be quiet!" Shouted my captor.

"What's your name?" I asked.

"Me Figar," he replied primitively, and then he pointed to Suzy's captor and then Antoine's. "This Digo and that Wexl."

"Well, nice to meet you Figar, Digo and Wexl. Don't you get tired of doing things like this for Shelman? Didn't I see you drag Fred out of the gym back in Marley?"

"Yes," Figar nodded, "that our job. We the muscle."

There was no doubt about that. They were big and strong, that was for sure. But it was clear that they weren't very bright. Maybe I could outsmart them.

"So, do Digo and Wexl talk too, or are you the speaker of the grunts?"

"They talk too," answered Figar. Digo and Wexl nodded silently.

I was trying not to laugh. The situation was dire and there was a battle raging a few hundred feet away and our families were tied to trees somewhere on the other side of the forest. Suzy was scared and Antoine was useless - and yet, I found this whole exchange a little funny.

"Why you laugh?" Figar asked.

"I don't know," I said, "I just can't help myself. I mean, you just told me that your two co-grunts could speak - but you spoke for them. It's just a little amusing, that's all."

His eyebrows furled like he was trying to put something together.

"They know how speak."

"It's okay," I smirked, "I believe you. Now, back to what I was asking before...don't you wish you were down there fighting the good fight for the Legion?"

"You not know anything," he turned and grunted, walking in the direction of the campfire. He picked up a stick and poked at the nearly spent coals. Digo and Wexl followed and continued their silence as they joined Figar in tending to the fire.

"I'm serious," I called to him. "Don't you wish you could be down there fighting with your comrades. I know I wish I could. It beats being over here, in the middle of a bunch of trees with a dying fire and three bratty kids...doesn't it?"

"We have job to do...we do it."

"It just seems to me, that maybe Shelman doesn't respect you enough to let you fight, that's all."

This one did it. Figar stopped stabbing at the fire and raised his head. He looked at Digo and Wexl. Their minds were now working as one, finally putting the pieces of the puzzle together. And then all at once, they shrugged their shoulders, uttered a small grunt and went back to poking the coals.

After a few minutes of trying to revive the fire in silence, the flame faded, the coals smoked and the fire was gone. They couldn't even do that right.

I heard a rustling in the bushes just past where the fire had been, but it was too dark to see who it was. And then they lit up - a pair of eyes, red and bright.

"Figar, Digo, Wexl," came a familiar voice.

"Master," they said in unison as they dropped to one knee and lowered their heads.

"At ease," the voice said.

The three stood up.

"Having a little difficulty with the fire, I see."

I saw the outline of the figure move his hand in an upward motion and then bring his hand down toward the smoldering pit.

Flames shot up and the fire resumed burning brighter than it had before.

"Thank you, master," Figar cowered.

"Go fetch some more sticks, this fire won't burn forever."

Figar, Digo and Wexl ran off into the woods to fetch sticks, like dogs. When they left, the figure came into full view.

I felt a lump form in my throat. I was no longer feeling playful or relaxed.

Out of the shadow of the flames, stepped the one man who could destroy us all.

BIG TROUBLE

"Coby," Shelman said, stepping forward out of the shadow of the newly revived flames. "You really should be a little more careful when speaking to my men. They're going to start thinking I don't value them."

He walked over to the three of us and looked down. He loomed over us. The threat of our impending doom was right in front of us, forcing us to face him - or put our eyes in the dirt and cower.

I refused to cower. I stared right into his bright red eyes.

"It's very important to your future -" he started laughing as he turned toward the fire. "Actually, nothing's important to your future at this point. You have no future. Not the one you want, anyway."

Flannery and Zenu emerged from behind the fire wheeling a long glass tube with wires snaking around the outside.

"What are you talking about?" I questioned. "This isn't over yet."

"You're right," Shelman fired back, wheeling around and pointing his finger down at me. "It isn't over yet. We're just beginning."

"What are you going to do to us?" Suzy asked.

"The same thing we've already done with your families. In less than an hour you will be the newest members of the Fleshbot Legion. You will know power like you've never known before. Doesn't that sound...enticing?"

"No," I defied. "It sounds terrible. I would rather die than be a member of your clan."

"You fool," he said. "We are the most powerful creations ever made. No mere man can defeat us. Only we are capable of defeating ourselves."

"There's quite a few of your own who are trying to do just that, aren't there?"

Shelman nodded. He walked over to the glass tube and started hooking the wires up. He worked quickly. Clearly, he'd done this before.

"There are always individuals who disagree with leadership and what's best for the group. This may come as a surprise to you, young as you are."

He snapped the last wire into place and slowly walked back to where we were sitting. He crouched down, his eyes were just above mine now.

"And you see, they always lose."

"This time will be different," I said, refusing to back down. I looked right into his eyes. He was not going to defeat me.

"You are too young to understand what you're saying. You still think that the actions of a small group can be enough to alter the course of history. Well, let me tell you, Coby, they can't. By the time tonight is over, our Legion will be a few hundred members fewer. But we will have added twelve new members."

"That doesn't sound like very good math," Suzy spoke up.

"It's perfect math," Shelman said. "You simply have to consider the members we're losing. They didn't want to be part of this in the first place. We're not losing them tonight - we lost them a long time ago. Tonight is about eliminating the threat. So, you see, we are gaining more tonight than we are losing."

He placed his arm along the top of the glass tube and gave it two quick taps, the sound of his ring on the glass giving them extra emphasis.

"Who's going first?"

CONVERSION

The fire flared and gave us a start. An air pocket in a log must've caused it to crackle, but the way Shelman was looking at us, it might as well have been him.

"I said, 'who's first?'" He walked closer and took Suzy's hand in his own. Holding it gently, he brought it toward his face and began to study it. "Yes. You would make a terrific Fleshbot. You're strong and willing to do whatever it takes, even if it might end in your demise."

She pulled her hand back.

"I'll never be a good Fleshbot," she said. "I'd pull my life cord immediately."

"Trust me dear," Shelman said, sliding his hand up his shoulder, toward the crook of his neck, "it is very, very difficult to reach your own life cord. Most of our Converts have this reaction, and eventually give in to the life of power and invincibility. It's just easier that way."

"I'll have someone else pull it then," she said, unwilling to concede the point.

"Now, that would be interesting," Shelman stood up and looked down at Suzy. "Do you think you have it in you to kill someone?"

"No," Suzy said quickly.

"Then, Ms. Trudell, how could you be so selfish as to ask someone to do that to you?"

"I wouldn't die, I'd just go back to being a human."

"Well, what do you think that is?" Shelman laughed and crouched back down. He brought his face close to Suzy's staring her in the eyes. "To be human is to die. To be Fleshbot is to live forever. When you ask someone to pull your life cord, you are asking them to force you into a mortal life, a life destined for end. So, you see, it's a very selfish request."

"What about what you're doing?"

Shelman stood back up and walked over toward the Conversion chamber.

"What we're doing, young lady, is not selfish at all. Quite the contrary. What we are doing is helpful. We are allowing people to live their lives forever, so long as they can follow the Fleshbot code."

"What if that's not what they want? It's selfish to force them into the life that you think is right."

He nodded. I could see his tongue working back and forth beneath his lips while he thought. After a few seconds he offered his retort.

"You have a lot to learn about people. You see, my dear, people do not usually know what's best for them. They rely on outside forces to tell them what to do. They are too misguided and closed minded to make the choices that would result in their ultimate success and happiness. They have the innate ability to stand in their own way. So, Suzy, sometimes it takes an entity like us to come along and show them what they really need."

He walked back over to us and folded his arms across his chest.

"Most of them come along willingly. But then, some of them are like you, and we have to use any force necessary to get the job done."

"Use whatever force you need to," Suzy said. "I'm not going willingly."

"It's the intelligent ones who are often the dumbest when it comes to this sort of thing. They think they know it all."

Shelman stepped toward me. Then he crouched and grabbed my hair hard and pushed my head back against the tree trunk.

"Coby Collins, your friend needs you now, desperately. She needs you to talk some sense into her."

"No," I said.

He tightened his grip on my hair and I could feel my scalp start to burn. Stray pieces of hair fell onto my face.

"I said, talk some sense into your friend, or it's going to get very ugly for both of you."

"No," I said, again.

I was forced to stare up at the tree branches that hid the starry sky. He was pushing my head back hard. And then I felt a sharp pain go through my forearm.

"Tell her to do it, or I'll mash your arm into a bruised mess!"

"No!"

The pressure on my arm increased and it seemed like I couldn't hold out much longer.

"Tell her!"

"I'll never help you!"

That did it. He started to twist my arm clockwise, away from my body. As he twisted, he squeezed harder and harder. I felt tears well up in my eyes. My hair was tingling. I was breathing hard, just trying to get through this, wondering how far he would take it.

I closed my eyes now and tried to go to a place in my mind where this wasn't real, a place where I'd never even met a Fleshbot. My teeth pressed hard on each other and gradually my breathing slowed and steadied. I could hear him talking to me, but I couldn't make out what he was saying. And I didn't dare open my eyes to see.

Then, as fast as the pain had come - it was gone.

RELIEF

My arm was still throbbing, but the searing, unrelenting pressure that was crushing my forearm was gone. My hair still tingled a little, but the feeling of knives and metal pinning my head to the tree had subsided. What was going on here?

I tilted my head forward just a little, trying to gauge whether or not Shelman was still there. There was no resistance as I brought my head down and tucked it into my chest. My eyes were still closed...I was afraid to open them. I expected Shelman's booming voice would send me back to reality. But it didn't.

Had I done it? Had I finally, after ten years of trying, managed to go to a place in my mind that made pain go away? It'd never worked before. Every time I had to get a shot from the doctor, or fell off my bike, or got hit by my sister - the pain had still existed. But now, in my truest moment of need, I just closed my eyes and then...poof - the pain was going away.

"Coby?"

Who's voice was that? It was a man's voice, but it wasn't Shelman's. I was certain of that.

"Coby?"

It wasn't loud enough to be Flannery's, nor was it creepy enough to be Zenu's. It was too concerned sounding to be Figar, Digo, or Wexl?

"Are you alright? Can you open your eyes?"

I felt a light slap on the side of my face. *Here we go again,* I thought. Then a soft hand gently pushed my face away from my chest. Another hand settled below my chin, supporting my head. The stray pieces hair were being brushed away.

"Come on Coby," the voice said, accompanied by another light slap, "time to wake up."

I started to open my eyes. They fluttered at first and it was hard to see what I was looking at.

Then I heard Suzy's voice.

"It's okay, Coby. You can wake up now. It's safe, he's gone."

"Who's gone?" I felt myself ask, almost involuntarily.

"Open your eyes," said the man.

I was finally able to get them to stay open long enough to see what was going on. Fred was sitting in front of me, on two knees. He was holding my face and brushing pieces of hair away.

I looked around for Shelman. Where had he gone? How had this happened? How long had I been asleep?

"Where's Shelman?" I asked. And then panic set it. "Fred, you've got to get out of here before he comes back!"

"He's not coming back," Fred said. He was so calm about it.

"What do you mean he's not coming back?"

Fred pointed down toward the ground, where his knees were firmly planted. There was a pile of dust and smoke. And then Fred grinned, letting go of my face. He pulled out a knife and a long green cord.

"He's gone," he said.

"You..."

"Shelman's dead. The main head of the beast is gone."

I stared at Fred, unable to speak.

"Coby, we're almost home," he said hopefully. "It's almost over. We just have to get Zenu and Flannery and then we'll be free!"

As he finished saying this, the sounds of broken twigs and branches rang through the trees. Figar, Digo and Wexl were on their way back with wood for the fire.

"We've got to go," I said. "They're coming back!"

Fred stuffed Shelman's green life cord into the pocket of his pants and took one quick upward slice with his knife. It easily cut through the rope that was holding us captive against the tree.

"Hide," he ordered.

Suzy and I ran behind the tree. Antoine was still hunched over, very much in view of where the three grunts would be momentarily. Fred took off toward the Conversion chamber and crouched down behind it.

"We have to get Antoine," I said to Suzy.

We ran around to the front of the tree again, hoping not to be seen. I grabbed Antoine's feet and Suzy grabbed his shoulders.

"We back!" came Figar's primitive voice from the trees. "We got fire wood for you."

Antoine was much heavier than I thought he would be. He was not a fat kid, really kind of scrawny if you ask me. But he wasn't exactly helping us move him. He just lay there limp. Suzy and I were able to get him about halfway around the tree when we heard Digo cry out.

"They get away!"

"You get back here - Shelman be mad if you not here!" Figar ordered.

I was caught somewhere between fear and bravado. I knew Fred was in a good hiding spot, and I figured it wouldn't be too much longer before he pounced.

"I don't think you have to worry about Shelman anymore," I said.

"What you mean?"

"He's gone."

"Where he go to?"

"I don't really know," I said, "but he definitely won't be back."

I looked over to the Conversion chamber, hoping that Fred was still there, and that he would come lunging out at any minute to take care of these three clowns. But he was gone.

Where did he go? I thought. *He was just there.*

"We have orders," said Figar. "Whether Shelman here or not. We have orders from Flannery and Zenu. We not to let you three go."

He rushed us. Suzy and I had to leave Antoine where he was and run to the other side of the tree.

"What do we do?" She asked.

"I don't know," I said. "I was kind of counting on Fred to get us out of this one."

"Me too."

"We run," I said, "in opposite directions. We get to a hiding spot and wait until it's safe to come out."

"Okay," she said. "I'll go that way." She pointed toward the cabins and the water.

"I'll go this way," I said pointing deeper into the woods. I would have rather gone toward the water, but I figured there'd be enough trees and brush to keep me hidden from view of any Fleshbots.

"What about Antoine?" she said.

"Leave him," I said. "He's not going to fight back, so they'll probably just tie him back up and wait for Shelman."

She nodded.

"I'll see you when this is all over," I said. "Good luck."

"You too."

Figar made his way over to us and Suzy took flight. She ran fast down the hill and I could see Wexl taking chase. It looked like she would get to the water before he could catch her. I turned the other way and had Figar chasing me. Digo stayed behind to make sure Antoine was secured.

I ran faster than I'd ever run before. I was weak, and tired, and hungry, and just plain sick of this. But when you're running for your life, it's best not to think about such things.

Surprisingly, I was faster than Figar. He was very large and very strong, but slow. I started to pull away and then found the biggest tree I could find to hide behind. The darkness worked in my favor. In a few hours the sun would be rising and hiding would become difficult, but it was easy at this point in the night.

I stood as quietly as I could and tried to temper my breathing. I'm sure my breaths must've been very loud, and in a quiet room, I'd stand out, but Figar was breathing heavier than I was. He finally caught up to me and then kept running right on past the tree I was behind.

I had told Suzy to stay put, but that's not what I was going to do. With two grunts out of the equation and Shelman no longer a threat, I had something else on my mind.

DUST

I took my time walking back. I was tired. I was also pretty sure that Antoine wasn't putting up much of a fight, so they'd more than likely just leave him alone.

It gave me a chance to think about things and catch my breath. I was wondering why Fred didn't come out and take care of the grunts the way he'd taken care of Shelman. It seemed like it would have been so easy. But he'd just disappeared. Something didn't seem right about that. It wasn't like Fred to disappear from a fight.

It occurred to me that, perhaps, he didn't disappear on his own. Was it possible that he was captured? If he was captured, who was it? And where did they take him?

An uneasy feeling started to creep into my stomach. I picked up my pace a little. And before I knew it, I was in a full run again. I was exhausted, but the thought of Antoine and Fred held captive and ready for Conversion was enough to get me moving.

Fred had already been Converted, and then unConverted. What would they do with him now? I doubted that they would just make him a Fleshbot again. I didn't want to think about it.

When I got back to the tree that we'd been tied to, Antoine wasn't there. I looked around for any sign that Antoine was nearby.

The fire had died down, the ropes were gone, and the Conversion chamber was no where to be found. I looked at the base of the oak and saw that Shelman was still a pile of dust. That was reassuring.

"Antoine," I yelled out in a shouted whisper. "Antoine?"

I got no answer.

I looked down toward the water. Suzy was standing knee high along the shore line, with her arms folded. She'd been wrapped in a blanket and was being consoled by a woman who had been in the cabin we'd come into when we arrived at Bale. It was nice to know that Suzy was okay. That was one less thing to worry about.

I walked over to the dust that was once Shelman. I crouched down and looked hard. It was just dust, sitting there on the leaves and muck. It looked like something my mom would've placed in the trash can when she was finished sweeping the floors or vacuuming the living room.

Yet, this pile of dust represented the existence of a creature so vile and so powerful. It made me shudder. Even though he was gone and his reign was over, it felt like he could just reemerge from this pile at any time. It seemed like he would come back more powerful than before. And this time, instead of striving for Conversion of the entire human race, he would come back with revenge on his mind. It wouldn't be enough for him to 'help' humans anymore. If he were to come back, he would want to destroy us.

I looked at that pile of dust, wanting to kick it and spit on it and do everything I could to ensure that he never came back. But my mother and father had taught me better than that. I took one last look at the pile and walked away, past the fire and into the heart of the forest, where the battle for Fleshbot supremacy was just getting started.

MORE TREES, MORE ROPE

The choice was this: Either move toward the clearing where the battle was raging and risk capture, or walk parallel to the water through the trees and remain concealed from view.

I chose to stay in the woods, using the trees as my cover. I stopped behind a tree for just a moment and took a glance toward the clearing. It was difficult to see exactly what was going on through the puffs of smoke and piles of dust. Who was winning? Could there be a winner?

After a few moments I forced myself to look away and focus on getting Antoine back. If I could find the Conversion chamber, I would find him.

I trotted along for a good five minutes, trying not to crack any twigs or branches beneath my feet, ducking behind tree after tree, giving myself cover and time to look around.

And then I heard it. I stopped. My ears perked and I looked in the direction of the noise. It was a hissing sound, like a loud snake. It came from deep within the woods. I noticed a stream of smoky vapor rising to touch the low hanging leaves of the trees.

Walking in that direction I could feel my palms become sweaty. I was about ready to vomit. This was the moment. Antoine was in here and that noise I was hearing was the Conversion chamber being fired up.

As I walked closer they came into view. Figar, Digo and Wexl were hard at work building another fire. Antoine was tied to a tree, sitting peacefully on the ground. Fred was tied to another tree. He was not sitting peacefully. His body was upright and his head was drooped over his shoulder. He had bruises on his face and arms and jagged pieces of hair adorned his shirt.

"My boy!" Flannery bellowed, giving me a start.

I wasn't able to see him yet. Where was he?

"You must wake up if this is going to work."

He walked out from behind the Conversion chamber and over to where Antoine was sitting. He grabbed his face in his hand. He lifted his head up, so Antoine was facing skyward, then he let go suddenly and let Antoine's chin bounce hard off his chest.

Antoine shook his head and opened his eyes. He moved his head from side to side like he was trying to work some stiffness from his neck. He looked up at Flannery and the glazed look came back.

"You?" he said.

"That's right, my boy! It's me. Are you ready to continue with our little project?"

"What do you mean?" He hadn't been conscious when Shelman had told us what the plan was. This caught Flannery slightly off guard.

"What do you mean, 'what do you mean'? Weren't you made aware of the plan and procedures for the evening?"

"No...I don't think so."

I had to get over to Fred. If I could grab the knife from his pocket, then maybe I could sneak up behind Flannery and cut his life cord.

I started moving around the makeshift Conversion site, quietly moving from tree to tree. Figar, Digo and Wexl were preoccupied with the fire and Flannery was busy trying to explain everything to Antoine.

I made it to Fred undetected. I tapped along the pockets of his pants, trying to feel for the knife. The only thing I felt was Shelman's life cord. The knife was gone.

Flannery made a move back to the Conversion chamber and moved a few switches and pushed some buttons. I saw something shining in the back pocket of his pants. It was Fred's knife. This made things a little harder.

There was no way I was going to be able to grab the knife and cut his life cord. He'd surely stop me and tie me up to a tree...or worse.

I remembered what Fred had said at the beginning of the battle. 'If you can't cut their life cords, just lunge and rip them from their power box.'

Flannery was still busily tending to the Conversion chamber. I took a good look, trying to see where his life cord might be located. I saw it. It was at the base of his neck and it ran down his back, the outline of it visible through his shirt.

Before I knew what I was doing, I was in a full sprint running hard at Flannery. As I got closer I positioned my hand and jumped into the air. I had to be sure that I grabbed what I needed to grab. If I didn't, Flannery would surely toss me into the Conversion chamber and I would be a Fleshbot forever.

Figar saw me and yelled a warning. "Watch out!"

This actually worked in my favor. Flannery turned for just a second and stared at Figar like he'd done something wrong. The way a master looks at his dog when he's training it.

Before he could look my way, I had the cord in my hand and I was on my way back down to the ground. My weight was enough to dislodge the cord and send Flannery up in a cloud of smoke and dust.

Figar, Digo and Wexl started running in my direction.

"You better run! Or we get you!"

I looked down at the dust that had been Flannery. The shiny blade of Fred's knife was visible. I reached down and picked it up and then held it out toward the three grunts.

"Don't come another step!"

They stopped and looked at each other, puzzled.

"Put knife down now," Figar commanded.

I kept the knife up and started walking backwards slowly.

"Put knife down!"

"Hold your horses," I said. "I've gotta do something first."

I reached my arm behind me and turned my head slightly to my left. Out of the corner of my eye I could see Fred. I continued to move in his direction. It wouldn't be long now...just a few more steps.

"Coby, um, you should really, um, stop and think about what you're about to do."

It was Zenu!

I looked around frantically. I couldn't see him anywhere. The grunts were pressing forward and moving in my direction once again.

"Zenu," I said, "Where are you?"

"I'm here," he said.

I needed to get Fred loose before the grunts got their hands on me and Zenu came out from wherever he was hiding.

I got to the tree and took the knife to the rope that was holding Fred up. His head was still resting on his shoulder.

I started to cut the rope. It took quite a lot of effort to get the knife through.

The rope started to fray.

"I wouldn't, um, do that if I were you."

"Well, you're not me," I said, continuing to cut.

"Very well. Figar, Digo - go get him and throw him right in the chamber!"

Figar and Digo began walking even faster than before.

They were just about to me when the rope snapped under the pressure of the knife. Fred fell to the ground. The jolt woke him up. He was groggy, but when he saw Figar and Digo heading in our direction he was able to shake off the cobwebs quickly.

He lunged at Digo and the two were instantly grappling, trying to work around each other for position. Fred was trying desperately to work his way around to Digo's back. Figar continued to move in my direction.

I made a move toward Antoine. I had to get him untied while I still had the knife in my hands.

As I moved toward the tree, Zenu stepped out of it's shadow and stood right in front of me.

"I told you not to do that."

ANTOINE'S CONVERSION

Fred looked to be getting the upper hand on Digo. He had gotten around the side of him and was now making his first attempts to grab at his life cord.

The first few missed. But on the third try he held it in his hand. He looked Digo in the face.

"How old are you?"

"Thirty," replied Digo. He looked confused by this question. But I knew exactly what Fred was doing.

"I'm going to pull this cord," Fred said. "And when I do, you're going to black out for a little while. When you finally come to, I'll be here and we'll join forces."

"I never join forces-"

Fred pulled hard and Digo's eyes gave a quick flutter and then he fell to the ground harmlessly.

Figar had stopped to watch what was happening.

As I looked back to him, I noticed someone coming up from behind. It happened quickly. But, just as Digo's body had gone limp a moment earlier, now so did Figar.

I turned back to look for Wexl, but he was already on the ground.

Stepping out of the shadows were two large men.

"Ballistrate...Rigger!" Fred was excited to see them. "What took you so long?"

"It's hard to see out here," said the man who'd just taken out Figar.

"That's just like you Balli, always making excuses."

The two men shared a chuckle and then shook hands and hugged each other, with hearty pats on the back.

"And Riggi," he said, turning to the other one, "how've you been, my good friend?"

"Good, good," replied Rigger.

I turned to look around, just in time to see Zenu dragging Antoine toward the Conversion chamber. Antoine was putting up a fight, but Zenu looked to be too strong for him.

In all the commotion, I had almost forgotten about Zenu.

"Guys," I said, "look!"

The three stopped their reunion banter and looked toward the chamber.

"Let him go," said Fred.

"It's a little late for that," Zenu said.

Wrestling Antoine, he picked him up and threw him into the chamber. Antoine was kicking and punching, but Zenu, for as frail as he appeared, was quite strong. He closed the top of the chamber and pushed Antoine's feet back inside just before the lid came down and latched.

"Just a few more moments now."

I could see the fear in Antoine's eyes. He was looking toward us for help. It was just a matter of time now and my best friend was going to become an enemy.

Zenu rushed around to the back of the chamber. Fred, Ballistrate and Rigger made a run at him. Zenu was frantically pushing buttons and the chamber lit up and a deafening whir stopped them in their tracks, momentarily.

"It's all over now!" Zenu said as he pushed the final button and ran deeper into the forest. Ballistrate and Rigger took chase.

Fred and I examined the control panel of the chamber. Neither one of us knew how to stop it. The whirring noise was going faster and faster and then the light inside the chamber became so bright, I could not see Antoine anymore. He was just a few feet away, but the light blanketed him.

"What do we do?" I yelled, trying to get my voice above the chamber.

Fred yelled something back to me, but I couldn't hear it.

"What?"

I looked at Fred's face. I couldn't hear what he was saying, but I was able to read his lips. What he said was the last thing I wanted to hear.

"We wait."

He was right. There was nothing we could do but wait. Except, that was not just some random human in there - it was Antoine. But I guess that's precisely why it was important to wait. If we were to start pressing buttons, not knowing what we were doing, it was very possible that Antoine could've become something worse than a Fleshbot.

"What do we do when he comes out?" I asked.

"Pull his life cord," Fred answered matter of factly. "But I must warn you, Coby. When your friend emerges, he will be very, very strong. I will have to take care of him. And you may not want to be here when that happens."

"I'm not leaving Antoine," I said.

"You need to, I'm afraid."

I know Fred was trying to protect me. He didn't want me to watch my friend 'die' and come back to life. That's the type of stuff that would mess a kid up. Deep down I knew this. But I also knew that Antoine was my best friend and I wanted to be there to help him, even if that help meant killing him as a Fleshbot so he could come back to life as my friend.

The chamber became quiet and all the light that had flooded the woods retreated. Antoine was lying on his back. He was staring straight up to the sky, his eyes glowing red.

"Get out of here, Coby. Work on getting to your family."

"What about Antoine?"

"I'll take care of him and bring him to you...trust me."

I looked into his eyes. He nodded.

"Okay," I said.

Reluctantly, I left to go find my family.

FAMILY

I ran through the trees, away from the Conversion chamber, and to the edge of the woods. I stopped, momentarily. I looked back just as Fred was ripping Antoine's life cord. Antoine fell to the ground like a rag doll.

He'd be okay. I had to keep telling myself these words so I could do what I had to do.

I moved forward once again, each step bringing me closer to the battleground. I could see the bottom of the clearing, just in front of the cabins. It was littered with piles of dust and listless bodies.

Suzy was still in the water. She was just standing there, watching everything unfold. The water was only up to her knees, but that was enough to keep her safe. She kept glancing up toward the tree line. No doubt, looking at her family, just waiting for the right moment to make her move.

When I arrived at the tree line I was surprised to see that everyone was awake. Suzy's mom and dad were looking around and staring out toward the water where Suzy was standing. Jenny's eyes were open, but I think she was in a similar state of shock as Antoine.

Antoine's parents looked horrified. How was I going to try to explain to them what was happening with Antoine? It would probably send them over the edge.

I turned to look at my parents and Jill. They, like the others were watching with some mixture of horror and curiosity.

It was clear that none of them had been moved. They were tied up and sitting exactly as they were at the start of the battle. This meant that they hadn't been Converted!

I ran over to my mom and dad. I gave them a huge hug. They started a little.

"Coby!"

I could feel their bodies relax as my presence set in. Jill called to me.

"Coby, what is this place?"

"I'm not sure exactly. And even if I did know, I don't think I'd be able to explain it right now." I moved toward the rope that wrapped around the tree and held my family into place. Pulling Fred's knife from my pocket, I went to work.

"We have to get out of here," I said.

"Where are we going to go?" my mother asked.

I pointed past the cabins toward the water. They took a moment to survey the field where the battle was still very much alive. She shook her head.

"Mom, you need to listen. We're going to the water. That's where we'll be safe."

The rope came loose and the three of them stood up. They were stiff and sore, as one might be if they were tied to a tree for who knows how long?

I moved next to Antoine's parents.

"Where's Antoine?" his father asked. "Where's our boy?" his mother echoed.

"He'll be okay," I said, trying to be reassuring but not knowing the best way.

I cut their ropes and they joined my parents.

Suzy's family was next. I cut them loose.

Suzy's dad pointed toward the water where Suzy was standing. "We're going down there? We're going to go see Suzy?"

"That's the plan," I said.

"What about Antoine?" Antoine's mother said. "I'm not going anywhere without my baby."

"He's in good hands," I said, half trying to convince myself that I'd made the right choice.

We started to head down when I heard a voice screaming through the trees.

"Wait! Coby, wait!"

FRED'S MOMENT

I knew that voice for sure. It was Fred. But why would he be telling me to wait? He was the one who told me to get to the water when I could.

I turned to see he was walking with Ballistrate and Rigger. He was holding two life cords in the air.

One of them had definitely belonged to Antoine, who'd come into view, running up from behind Fred, to take a spot on his left.

But who had the other life cord belonged to?

"We got him Coby!" And then he stopped and looked at Balli and Riggi. "Well...they got him! Zenu's dead. The final piece of the head. Now we can make it known that their leaders are gone and not coming back!"

"Excuse me," said Antoine's mother, "but who is this man walking with my son, talking about heads and death?"

"Oh, it's okay," I said. This must've looked very strange to her. "These men saved Suzy, Antoine and me. They are good guys."

Antoine ran up and gave his mother and father a hug and all arguments from his parents ceased.

Suzy's parents were standing off to the side. "When do we get to see our girl?"

"Soon," said Fred. "Very soon. There's just one thing I have to do."

He looked around the ground muttering to himself, "it has to be around here somewhere."

"What are you looking for?" Suzy's father asked.

"I'm looking for - ah, there it is." Fred bent over and picked something up off the ground. "I've been waiting a long time for this."

He brought Shelman's bullhorn up to his lips.

"Halt!" he yelled.

It took a few moments for everyone to stop fighting. A few of the Fleshbots stopped early and were quickly turned to dust.

Once everyone had stopped and had their eyes on Fred, he continued.

"The Legion is dead!"

About half of those left on the battlefield cheered wildly. Raising their arms high and letting out jubilant cries.

"Shelman is gone! Flannery is gone! And Zenu is gone!"

The group of Fleshbots that weren't cheering looked like a child who'd just had his favorite toy taken away. They were disappointed and lost.

A few of them started to run. They took off in different directions, clearly in no mood to fight now. After the first wave left, a second and third group went on their ways. They all went in different directions as well.

Some of Fred's group started to run after them.

"Stop! Stay where you are," he commanded through the bullhorn. "We will regroup. And then we will chase and destroy. But we will be united first."

There looked to be about a hundred or so left, once everyone else had left.

"Go to the middle cabin and we will decide how to proceed."

They did as they were told. Fred turned to Ballistrate and Rigger. "Get them set up. Make sure the map is there."

"Yes, sir." They ran down toward the middle cabin and were inside within a minute.

I looked toward the water where I thought Suzy would be standing. She had left the water when she saw the Fleshbots scatter. She was now headed toward us, running fast toward her family.

Fred turned and looked at me.

"Thank you, Coby. You saved my life."

"Likewise," I said.

He turned toward our parents. "Your children are very brave. No doubt they learned their values from you."

"We try," my mother said. Antoine's parents nodded. Suzy's parents were too busy hugging Suzy to pay attention to what Fred was saying.

"You folks should go home now. We can handle this job from here. It'll be much easier without the Legion Leadership in place. Rest assured, we'll take care of things."

Fred put his hand out. I put my hand out and we shook hands.

"It's been an honor to know you." And with that, Fred

walked down to the cabin to organize his party.

IT'S OVER

I gave my mom and dad and Jill the biggest hug I'd ever given them.

Antoine and Suzy were hugging their parents as well. We remained locked in these embraces for several minutes before walking down toward the water.

As we made our way, I noticed the piles of dust everywhere.

How many had died tonight? Too many, I suppose.

The sun was starting to rise. The clouds over the water were dark, but they'd lighten up soon enough.

I led my family out to a rocky pier that reached out into the water.

Suzy and Antoine came up and stood next to me.

"That's quite a boy you have there," I heard Suzy's dad tell my parents.

"That's quite a girl you have there," my father replied, and then turning to Antoine's parents, "I've always liked your boy, too. He's a great friend to Coby."

It was awkward, but aren't moments like this always that way.

When you go through something like we'd just been through, there's so much of it that you want to tell people about. So much that you want to share, and yet, I didn't feel like talking. And neither did Suzy, nor

Antoine. Our parents were exchanging niceties, but they really didn't want speak either.

I just kept looking out at the water. They waves were slowly brushing over the rocks along the shoreline. It wasn't settled, but it was calm. I could relate. There was so much going on inside of me. There was so much of my journey that I would like to forget. But I had a feeling that those were the things I wouldn't ever be able to truly let go. I would have to work hard just to live with those memories.

I could feel it churning inside of me. And then I began to cry. I cupped my hands around my face and sat down on the ground. It was my sister, Jill, who came over and put her arm around me.

"It's okay," she whispered into my ear. "It's over."

I pulled my head out of my hands and gave her a knowing nod. But it didn't make the pain any less. My memories of them and the marks that they'd left on my life would remain forever.

Antoine and Suzy sat down next to me. We held hands and looked out across the water. I didn't really know what they were thinking. Perhaps they weren't thinking. Perhaps they were just taking the opportunity to enjoy the silence. That's what I was doing, anyway.

Suzy's sister, Jenny, came over and sat on Suzy's lap. Suzy took her free hand and wrapped it tightly around her.

"I'm never going to let you go," she said to Jenny.

"Never ever?"

"Never ever."

My father came over and tapped me on the shoulder.

"What d'ya think there, buddy?"

He paused after he said this. It was clear that he wanted to get going, but didn't rush me. He was anxious, but wanted to give me the time I needed.

"I haven't had anything to eat but a granola bar and some fruit snacks in two days," I said.

"Yeah," said Antoine, "I'm kinda hungry myself."

Everyone else agreed that they were famished as well. My sister pushed hard for The Taco Joint, but in the end, it was I who had the final choice.

We went to Matt's Pizza and Sub Shop in Marley. It was the best of both worlds. You could have pizza or a really big sandwich, both of which were fresh and tasted great. Neither of them had been wrapped in plastic or taken out of a freezer. It was wonderful. And, as you can imagine, I ate more than enough.

When all was said and done, our families went their own ways. I knew I would see Antoine, Suzy and Jenny at school on Monday. But for now, it was time to go home.

EPILOGUE

I'm an old man now.

With my remaining years at Marley, it was always a challenge to forget what I'd been through. What terrible things I'd seen.

Since that day in Bale, I have never seen another Fleshbot. My children, and their children have been left alone thus far.

We thought, when we left the pier and headed back to Marley, that all was over; that life could go back to normal.

And for us, it did.

But there were many, for whom, the nightmare was just beginning.

You see, that day in Bale, many Fleshbots were lost. But Shelman said once, that they'd taken up residence all over the country.

This is true.

I am relatively certain that no harm will come to my family, as it's been over 70 years since my last encounter with a Fleshbot. But I can be certain that others, such as yourself, might, one day come in contact with a living, breathing Fleshbot.

And when that day comes, I hope you remember my story. I hope you remember that they can be defeated, and that no battle is too big.

I hope that you can find the strength to dig in your heels, steal some courage and stand up for what you believe. Go forth, and make sure that your corner of the world is free from Fleshbots for as long as you and your families shall live.

SPECIAL SNEAK PEEK

Scab and Beads
P.S.I.
Playground Scene Investigation

Scabs is a goofball, who's obsessed with showing off his war wounds. Beads is a diva who makes her own jewelry.
Together they come together to form one of the most amazing elementary mystery solving teams since...ever!

IT'S LIKE CSI FOR KIDS!

(JUST TURN THE PAGE)

SCAB
AND
BEADS

PSI
PLAYGROUND SCENE INVESTIGATION

FREE PREVIEW
THE FIRST 5 CHAPTERS

JUSTIN
JOHNSON

Monday Afternoon
2:37 PM

The sun was high in the sky and the kids of Steven A. Mason Elementary School were happily playing outside.

Scabs was sitting at the far end of the playground on a hill, in the shade, with a group of first graders. He was notorious for sitting with the younger kids and showing them his latest...well, scabs.

"I got this one yesterday, so it's certified fresh," he said.

"What's certified mean?" one of the kids asked.

"It means 'genuine, or authentic,'" Scabs told the group. He knew this because he'd had to look the word up earlier in the day during a dictionary activity. He loved dictionary activities, but it often resulted in Scabs using words that his younger admirers didn't know.

"What's genuine mean?" asked another of the first graders.

"It means 'certified,' of course," answered Scabs, who had not had to look up the word genuine, and therefore had no idea what it meant.

"Oh, okay," said the kid, who gave a glassy eyed stare. This let Scabs know the boy had no idea what he was talking about and was only agreeing with him so they could get to the real reason everyone was gathered around.

"Now," Scabs continued, "if I may." He reached down toward his knee and grabbed the corner of a very large band aid. In fact, it was less a band aid and more of a full fledged patch. It covered his entire knee and wrapped around to the back of his leg.

The group of first graders consisted of about fifteen kids. Once Scabs reached for his knee, they started jockeying for position.

"Hey," Scabs said, "stop that nonsense! If you can't control yourselves then I'm going to stand up and walk over there." He pointed to the track, where most of his classmates were standing around talking. Of course, he had no intention of actually going over there. He felt he had far more to offer this group of eager first graders, than he could ever offer his fifth grade classmates. Besides, they didn't care about his scabs half as much as these seven year olds did.

Nonetheless, the kids stopped pushing and focused their gazes toward the right knee of Scabs.

He slowly peeled back the bandage, wincing and gritting his teeth for dramatic effect. Of course, this didn't hurt him. By this point in the day he'd removed his bandage no fewer than 37 times, so it was no longer sticky or clingy.

The first kid caught a glimpse of the half scabbed over, half bloody scrape and started to gag. Scabs had tried to take his bike off a home made ramp the night before. It had gone poorly, but wasn't that the point? Scabs was always putting himself in situations to get these little gems that made him the center of attention - at least for 10% of the first grade.

"It's okay, Roger," one of the first graders said to the boy. "Do you need to go to the nurse?"

Roger waived the kid off, "I'm okay."

For they knew that if Roger tossed his cookies the show would be over. It happened a few months earlier. Scabs was showing them a cut on his finger. His mother had put some kind of greenish yellow salve underneath the band aid that gave the cut the appearance of having an infection. Tasha Meddelman had just finished her snack and when Scabs pulled back the band aid, well, let's just say it was too much for Ms. Meddelman. Scabs had stood up and walked over to the track, leaving 10 or so first graders very disappointed. Tasha was not invited back to this corner of the playground, and was relegated to the swings and monkey bars as a consequence.

The bandage was almost fully removed, hanging on by just the last little section of sticky when a voice was heard behind the group.

"Alright guys, show's over!"

Scabs quickly patted the bandage down and the group turned to see Beads walking over from the track.

She was wearing a bright green T-shirt with a brand name logo and neon pink shorts that had the same logo on the left leg. She had boondogle bracelets dangling from her wrists and her hair was an intricate tapestry of thinly braided strands, each laced with it's own pattern of neon colored craft beads.

"Man," said a boy named Aidan. "You always do this! Just when he's getting to the best part, you stop him and make him leave."

Beads was cool. She wasn't going to let a first grader ruffle her feathers. She looked down at the boy, letting her craft beaded hair click clack as she said, "You're lucky I let him get that far."

This was enough to shut the boy up. She then looked at Scabs and raised her eyebrows in a hurrying fashion.

Scabs caught the vibe and stood up quickly.

"Well," he said, "it's been a pleasure. Thank you so much for your attention. We'll do the same thing next week...same time, same channel."

Beads rolled her eyes and threw her hair back. Scabs had picked up that saying from some radio show, or something, a few weeks back. It was annoying the first time he used it, but now it was border line unbearable.

Scabs turned his attention to Beads.

"What's up?" he asked.

"We've got a problem."

Monday Afternoon
2:53 PM

The two walked closely across the playground, legs in step with one another.

"What do you got?" Scab asked.

"Missing locket," replied Beads.

"To whom did it belong?"

"Ariana Frunderland."

"Doesn't she live in the apartments by the old Sell More?"

"That's the one," Beads said, her hair click clacking as she nodded.

"What level of importance does she give to the locket?" asked Scabs.

"Does it matter?" Beads said, turning her head to glare at Scabs. She thought he could be so insensitive at times. He was always trying to do this, get out of work by passing the job off as unimportant.

Scabs shrunk in his skin. "No, I guess it doesn't."

The two were just about halfway through the track's infield when a football whizzed by Beads's head.

"Excuse me," she said to Scabs. Then she took off on a dead sprint in the direction of the ball. She got to it before Joshua Jenkins, the boy who the pass had been intended for. He was laughing now, which would prove to be a costly mistake. For Scabs knew one thing about Beads, one truth that kept their relationship even keel - YOU DID NOT MESS WITH BEADS.

She picked the ball up and started swinging it in his face.

"Are you seriously laughing right now? Because, boy, if you are then I'm gonna take this football and throw it in those bushes over there!" She motioned to a spot just past the track that had a small, but noticeable overgrowth of leafy vegetation.

"Go ahead, that's no big deal," responded Joshua, trying not to look like he was having it handed to him by a girl...a girly girl nonetheless.

"Let's go Beads," said Scabs, trying to calm the situation down a little.

"You be quiet and stay over there," said Beads. "I'll call you when I need you. But I'm pretty sure I'm not going to need you."

"Just give me the ball," Joshua said. "Then we can get on with our game and you and your boyfriend can continue your little promenade."

"Oh, nice one," Beads said, turning back toward Scabs. "Dictionary activity this morning, right?"

"Yeah," Scabs said, "that was one of our words."

"My group didn't have that word," said Beads. She started walking toward the shrubbery with the football, still talking to Joshua. "You know what word we did have though?"

"No, what?"

"Poison Ivy," Beads said. "And that's what this bush is." She held the football about a foot over the bush, her tiny fingers looking as though they were about to lose their grip. "It would be a shame if I were to drop this, wouldn't it?"

"Look," said Joshua starting to come to his senses. "We didn't mean it. We had no idea that ball was going to fly so close to your head. Seriously, we're sorry. So you can just give us our ball back and we'll be on our way."

"Yeah," said Beads, "you see, I wish it was that easy."

"It is that easy," said Joey Darling. He was the boy who threw the ball, who until now had been silent about the whole matter, willing to let his friend, Josh, take the fall. But now that the ball - his ball - was in jeopardy of being inflicted with the blight known as Poison Ivy, well, he had to step in. "Just give us our ball back...or you can be certain of something like this happening again."

That was it. Something inside Beads snapped. She went on a verbal tirade.

"You really think that I'm just going to let you two get away with this whole thing? You must think I'm outta my mind. You must think this girl, Beads, is about as crazy as they come. Well, I'm not. In fact, I'm not crazy at all. But in a minute you're going to be thinking you're the crazy ones 'cause your ball is going to be buried in this Poison Ivy and one of you is gonna have to jump in and get it. And watching the two of you play ball and the decision that you made to throw the ball at me in the first place, well, that makes me think that at lease one of you is just dumb enough to do it. And then you'll get your ball, but you'll also have a wicked case of the itchies. Is it worth it?"

"Just give us the ball already," Joshua yelled desperately.

"Nope," said Beads. Her already sweaty fingers were starting to slip and the ball was almost out of her hand. She opened her fingers just a little bit more and the ball fell, seemingly in slow motion, into the Poison Ivy brush.

"Nooooooooooo!" yelled Josh and Joey in unison as they both ran up to the shrub and stopped short. Josh pushed Joey in saying, "Go get it. You threw it and it's your ball."

"I'm telling Mrs. Ruter," Joey yelled as he grabbed his ball and hopped out of the brush. He took off on a tear toward a group of teachers who were standing in the shade, talking. Joshua took chase, trying to get there before Joey.

Beads just laughed and looked at Scabs. "Are you ready to continue?"

"Was that really Poison Ivy?" Scabs asked.

Beads shrugged and smiled, "The world may never know."

"No, seriously, you can tell me."

"No. It wasn't Poison Ivy." Beads said rolling her eyes. "Honestly, I'm in the same class as both of you. You did the dictionary activity this morning, didn't you?"

"Yeah."

"Well, we share our words at the end. Poison Ivy wasn't on anyone's list. Didn't you pay attention?"

"No," said Scabs. They walked a few more steps and he asked, "So what is that bush then?"

"I don't know," Beads said. "It doesn't matter any how, we've got bigger issues."

"Right, Ariana's Locket."

"Correct."

"So, have you talked to Ariana yet?" Scabs asked.

"No."

"How did you hear about the locket?"

"My cousin is friends with Ariana," said Beads. "We had dinner last night at her house and she told me that Ariana was in a complete panic over the thing."

"Alright," said Scabs, rubbing the bandage that had come undone and was now blowing in the wind. He was trying to get it to stick back on his knee, but was having no luck. "What do we do now?"

"Well, for starters," Beads said, "You can take that silly bandage off your knee. It's not that bad and it'll heal better in the open air than it will under there. Just like most of your cuts would. Secondly, we need to find a way to talk to Ariana and see if we can get some leads on this investigation."

"Refresh my memory," Scabs said, continuing to smooth the bandage over, ignoring Beads's advice, "what's a lead?"

"It's like a clue. Something that would *lead* us in the right direction."

"Oh, yeah - got it." They walked a few more steps. Scabs could tell that Beads was deep in thought, but wasn't quite sure what about. "What are you thinking about?"

Beads stopped and turned to face Scabs. "The same thing you're supposed to be thinking about right now…how are we going to arrange our schedules so that we can speak to Ariana about her locket? Don't you listen to anything I say?"

"Sure I do," Scabs said defensively. "It's not that I wasn't listening, it's that I didn't understand what you were talking about."

Beads rolled her eyes and click clacked a little faster than Scabs was ready for.

"Would you be okay with it if I went to the nurse and asked for another bandage?"

Beads stopped walking and turned on a dime. She walked right back to where Scabs was standing and stood toe to toe with him, looking him straight in the eyes.

"I told you already, let it heal on its own," she said through gritted teeth. "Besides, you have to help me figure out how we're going to get a chance to talk to Ariana."

She turned away from him and kept walking fast.

"Right," Scabs said, a little forlorn. He put his head down and kept walking, trying to act like he was thinking about Ariana and her locket. But all he was really thinking about was how he was going to have to wait until he got home to put a new bandage on his knee…and what a long afternoon it was going to be.

Monday Evening
5:51 PM

After dinner Scabs headed over to Beads's house for a little post supper think session. It was time to do some serious figuring. The question in question: How to talk with Ariana Frunderland by herself, about the locket?

This was going to be a doozy. If they could talk to her, it would open up the doors to so many possibilities. But Ariana was a third grader and Scabs and Beads were in fifth grade. Their schedules didn't allow for any shared free times. It would take some planning.

"Come on in, Stanley," Scabs was greeted by Beads's mother, Mrs. Nelson. He hated it when people called him Stanley. He liked to be called Scabs - and only Scabs. He'd even gotten his teacher to stop calling him Stanley for crying out loud.

"Thank you, Mrs. Nelson," Scabs returned politely as he crossed the threshold.

Mrs. Nelson called up the stairs to Beads, "Miranda, your friend Stanley is here."

A very grumpy Beads called down. "Mom! I've told you, I'm not Miranda - I'm Beads...and he's not Stanley - He's Scabs!"

"Terribly sorry," her mother said insincerely. She turned back toward Scabs and put on a fake smile. "Miranda will see you now, Stanley."

Scabs walked up the stairs and turned right to go into Beads's bedroom. It was a total girly room. The walls were painted pink and she had posters of her favorite popstars plastered all over. Little frilly sheets adorned her four poster bed and there was lace draped from one post to the next.

Beads sat over in the corner at her jewelry table. She was working on what looked to be her latest bracelet. Looking through a magnifying light, she used a small set of forceps to feed bead after bead onto a length of thread.

"Come in and sit down," she said without looking up. "We have a lot to do."

Scabs pulled a rubber ball from his pocket and plopped, stomach first, onto the bed, his feet dangling off one side, his arms and head off the other. He slowly and rhythmically began bouncing the ball off the floor and catching it, and bouncing it and catching it.

"That's going to drive me nuts," said Beads, still not looking up.

"It's how I think," said Scabs.

"Don't give me that," Beads snarled, "I've seen you come over here and bounce that ball before. It never gave you any great ideas."

"Well, I like it."

"Well, that's a different thing, now isn't it?"

"Yeah, so?"

"So," said Beads, turning her chair now, a purple bead in her forceps, "I feed beads onto beading thread because it helps put my mind in a place where it can be productive. You bounce your ball and say that your mind is productive...but really you just 'like it'. Meanwhile, I get ever more annoyed with you and my mind becomes distracted and my thinking becomes fallible."

"What's fallible?"

"Last week's dictionary activity. Honestly, Scabs, you should really try to hold onto these words for longer than a day. It means that I'm liable to make a mistake. So, put the ball away please and do something that will make your mind more productive."

"It's okay," Scabs said, continuing to bounce the ball, "this'll work."

Beads sucked in a breath of air and then exhaled it slowly. Then she turned back to her bracelet making.

The two sat there in silence for several minutes, Scabs bounced his ball and Beads fed her beads. Then Scabs had an idea.

"I've got it!"

"What's that?"

"Maybe we don't have to figure out a time to see Ariana at school."

"What do you mean?" Beads asked, cocking her head over her right shoulder, trying to understand.

"I mean, maybe we go to her house...tonight."

Beads put down her almost finished bracelet carefully and began stroking her chin with her thumb and forefinger.

"This has promise," she said. She looked out the window, through purple curtains and noted that it was not yet dark. "Yes, this has a great deal of promise."

Scabs went back to bouncing his ball. He knew this would take Beads a few minutes to work through. She didn't like making mistakes and therefore, was extremely deliberate, even over the most minute of decisions.

"Let's see," said Beads, "her house is just about three minutes from here on bike. Did you ride your bike over?"

"Yes."

"Okay. And it's 6:00 now. What time do you have to be home?"

"My mom said no later than 7:00."

"That sounds good. So, if we leave now and account for the fact that it'll take us five minutes to tell my parents where we're going and another three minutes to get over there...let's see that means we'll be there by 6:08. If you have to be home by 7:00 then you should probably leave her house by 6:55. Let's factor in that her parents are going to want to know why we're there and we'll have to spend a few minutes talking to them. That should give us," she looked at the ceiling and moved a few fingers back and forth to signal her computation, "43 minutes! That'll be just enough time to get most of the information we need."

Scabs stood up and walked over to Beads. "That's the power of the bounce," he said proudly, holding the ball out in front of him for effect before putting it in his pocket.

"Well, if it leads to ideas like this," Beads smiled, "bounce away!"

Beads turned off her jewelry making lamp and the two walked downstairs to spend five minutes talking with Beads's parents.

Monday Evening
6:10 PM

It took them much longer than five minutes to convince Beads's mom to let her ride her bike over to Ariana's house.

"It'll be dark soon," her mother said.

"I'll be careful," Beads argued.

"I don't know, Miranda. It really isn't a very safe thing to do."

This was a rare occasion. Beads almost always got her way and was usually able to think around any situation, without resorting to tactics that would seem childish or undignified. But tonight, whether she was tired, or just plain out of ideas, things were different. Beads proceeded to beg.

"Pleeeeaaaase mom, pleeeeaaaase? I have to go. This is super important."

Her mother rolled her eyes and looked up toward the ceiling. She looked up there for a long time. Scabs found himself looking up there too, just to see what she was looking at. He didn't see anything and figured that she must've just been trying to figure out a way to tell Beads 'no.' But before she could do this, Beads hit her with the clincher. The lie that every child tells their parent when something's really important and it seems like the most important thing in the world, at least for that moment. And it's not a lie per se, but more of an empty promise. Because the child really means it in that moment - they just don't realize that in a day, or week, or month, something equally as important will come up and they will find themselves saying the exact same thing.

Beads said, "Mom, I promise - I will never ask for another thing as long as I live. Never again, I swear!"

And as Beads expected, her mother said, "Fine. But be home by 7:00."

"I will," Beads said, jumping up and down and giving her mother a hug. "Love you, see you later."

She ran to the back of her house to get her bike out of the garage. When she returned, Scabs found himself with a case of bike envy. They almost never went anywhere together on their bikes and this was only the second or third time Scabs had ever seen it.

It was amazing. Beads rode a boys mountain bike. The frame was a dark, metallic blue and, contrary to Scabs's beat up old bike, there wasn't a scratch anywhere to be seen. She had a custom, wide bottomed seat, that made for a far more comfortable ride than Scab's narrow stock option. The front handlebars had brand new, neon grips that had ergonomically designed grooves, designed to fit the hands perfectly. Scabs had fallen off his bike so many times that his handle bar grips had been worn down considerably. The left one, sporting a slit that spanned the entire length of the grip, looked as though it would fall off at any moment. The piece de resistance of Beads's wondrous piece of high tech machinery, was the gear system. Her bike had three gear shifters, each one controlling six of the possible eighteen speeds her bike was capable of.

"You ready?" Beads said, sliding on her neon pink helmet. It had black accent lines that were meant to give the illusion of flowers. She was stylish, if nothing else.

"Yeah," Scabs replied as he plunked his helmet onto his head. His helmet was a dull black that was full of little white and brown nicks and scrapes. He used to have a red sticker design of a dragon on the sides, but he'd fallen so many times it had worn off.

Together, they pushed off the sidewalk and into the flow of traffic - with five minutes less then they'd planned.

Ariana Frunderland was sitting on the front stoop of her apartment. Other kids were playing in the courtyard. There was a basketball game going on in one corner, some kids playing catch with a baseball in another, and a group of skateboarders and rollerbladers attempting to do tricks in the middle. If they had been a little younger, one might have thought they were part of the Scabs Fan Club. However, they looked to be in middle school and would definitely not meet the age requirement.

Cindy Warring and Julie Thomas were each holding one end of a jump rope and twirling it over the head and below the feet of a girl named Shelly Summers. Shelly was good, really good. She never missed a jump and was able to do fancy tricks. She was a fourth grader and Ariana looked at her admiringly. She knew that she would never be able to land a cartwheel, all the while keeping the jump rope from becoming tangled, like Shelly could. But she did hope that someday she would be able to jump rope on one leg.

The girls had asked her a half hour earlier if she'd like to give it a try. She'd said no. Not because she didn't think she could measure up to Shelly...let's face it, nobody could. Cindy and Julie were two years older than Shelly and had only half of her skipping skills. Ariana had said 'no' because her mind was elsewhere.

She stared off into space, allowing the noise to come in and out of her ears, never registering exactly what the sound was. She'd watched the boys and girls move back and forth at their games, yet her eyes never allowed them to come into focus. She was thinking of one thing - and that one thing was at the front of her mind, just as it had been since the moment it had been given to her by her Grandmother Nipsy before she'd died. Her silver locket.

The locket that had once adorned her neck was missing. She knew it was irrational to think that because she'd lost the locket, which housed the only picture of her with her Grandma Nipsy, that she'd also lost any connection with her grandmother at all. She knew she had the memories of the time they'd spent together reading books, and playing board games, and baking cookies, and those special 'secret' trips to the ice cream truck. But she worried that one day she would not be able to remember what her grandmother had looked like. She feared that she'd forget. And now, as she sat here on the stoop, barely aware of everyone going on with their day as though nothing had happened, the image of her grandmother in her locket was as vivid as ever.

The picture was taken down at Miller's Campground and RV Park. It was a favorite place for them to go. Ariana's family didn't have a lot of money and camping in a tent was only a few dollars for the weekend. She and her grandmother would often steal away from the rest of the family and go for walks down by the water. That's where the photo was taken - on the shore of Lake Kerrigan.

Before she had time to remember how her grandmother had jumped in the water with her clothes on just after the photo was taken, and how she'd dragged Ariana too, her thoughts were interrupted.

She noticed a click clacking noise that hadn't been present a moment earlier. Then she felt a shadow block the setting sun. As she brought her eyes into focus on the sidewalk she could see the black outlines of two people standing over her. She looked up squinting.

"Are you Ariana?" asked a girl with bright neon clothes and craft beads in her hair.

"Yes," she replied timidly.

"Can we go inside and talk?" asked the boy, who's arms and legs were covered in band aids.

"Why?"

The girl answered. "Let's just say, we're here to help."

ALSO COMING SOON

<u>Svenson Golding, Jr.</u>

Svenson Golding, Jr. comes from a long line of geniuses and successful business men. His father, Svenson, Sr. is the richest and most powerful man in the entire world.

But his fortune and power are being threatened by his boyhood friend turned foe – Dinglebert Lappity Lapp.

Dinglebert has spent the past twenty-five years living in a self-made tunnel, below a pre-fab shed, in the parking lot of a Home Depot. During that time he's been plotting his revenge...and now, it's time!

Can Svenson Golding, Jr. – the heir to the Golding fortune and professional booger eater – come through and save the day? Or will Dinglebert Lappity Lapp destroy the family business and exact his revenge?

ABOUT THE AUTHOR

Justin Johnson is a school teacher in Fulton, NY. He loves to write stories for his students as an end of the year gift. He lives in Hastings, NY with his family.

Go to www.justinjohnsonauthor.com to subscribe to my newsletter and get a free book.

Like Justin on Facebook @ www.facebook.com/jjohnsonauthor

To email Justin, send a line to: jjohnsonauthor@gmail.com

If you enjoyed this book, please rate it and write a review on amazon. And don't be afraid to tell a friend. Thank you very much!

Made in the USA
Middletown, DE
09 December 2015